EVE OF ETERNAL NIGHT

Trust No One

AMBER LYNN NATUSCH

Eve of Eternal Night
The Zodiac Curse: Harem of Shadows Book One
© 2018 Amber Lynn Natusch

All rights reserved. No portion of this book may be reproduced in any form without permission from the publisher, except as permitted by U.S. copyright law.

ISBN-13: 978-0-9998841-1-9

Eve of Eternal Night is a work of fiction. Names, characters, places, and incidents either are the products of the author's imagination or are used fictitiously. Any resemblance to actual persons, living or dead, businesses, companies, events, or locales is entirely coincidental.

Published by Amber Lynn Natusch
Cover by 99Designs
Paperback Formatting by Incandescent Phoenix Books
Editing by Kristy Bronner

http://amberlynnnatusch.com

ALSO BY AMBER LYNN NATUSCH

The *CAGED* Series

CAGED

HAUNTED

FRAMED

SCARRED

FRACTURED

TARNISHED

STRAYED

CONCEALED

BETRAYED

The *UNBORN* Series

UNBORN

UNSEEN

The *BLUE-EYED BOMB* Series

LIVE WIRE

KILLSWITCH

The *FORCE OF NATURE* Series

FROM THE ASHES

INTO THE STORM

BEYOND THE SHADOWS

Contemporary Romance

UNDERTOW

More Including Release Dates

amberlynnnatusch.com

www.facebook.com/AmberLynnNatusch

http://www.subscribepage.com/AmberLynnNatusch

To C.N. Crawford,

*Thanks for helping create
this crazy world with me.*

ACKNOWLEDGMENTS

Thank you to C.N. Crawford, Shannon Morton, Kristy Bronner, Kristi Massaro, Courtney DeLollis, Simone Nicole, Jena Gregoire, my ARC team, my family, and so many others for supporting me, believing in me, and indulging this crazy hobby-turned-career of mine. You're the best.

PROLOGUE

I felt her magic crushing me in place. Unable to move, I knew death was coming for me. The blade at my throat only confirmed that fact.

She stood behind me, allowing me a clear view of the carnage our war had caused. Bodies lay before me. The bodies of my men.

"It always comes down to this," she said, her voice sweet and sympathetic, belying her true nature. She was savage and brutal—just like me. I struggled against the magic bindings to no avail. "You know there is no escaping your destiny. To try only makes you look foolish." The dagger pressed harder against my skin, holding me still. "Until we meet again..."

Sadness overtook me as I stared into the vacant eyes of the men I loved—the men who had fought at my side—knowing that I had led them to their fate. Our fate. Then, with a tremendous blow and the sharp bite of steel, darkness took me.

I, too, was dead.

Again.

1

The bass throbbed, reverberating right through me. Red plastic cups riddled the floor—they made a satisfying crunch whenever I stepped on one. But not satisfying enough to distract me from the stench of stale beer and sweat that permeated the air. It was just like every other college party I'd been to, the Groundhog Day rite of passage for any co-ed. I wondered if I'd miss it when I graduated. Then I looked over at some idiot crushing a can against his forehead and knew I wouldn't.

Like really, *really* wouldn't.

I managed to find a spot somewhere off to the side of the humping masses, not wanting to be caught up in the middle of the 'dance floor'. I was good with not being felt up, some freshman looking at me like he was doing me a favor while he grabbed my ass. I didn't want to get arrested again, like last time. I didn't want Jim to have to come bail me out; Jim didn't enjoy that. Said it made him look bad, and how could I be so selfish, and did I want him to be in the papers again? In truth, I didn't give a shit. Jim—or Dad, as he insisted I call him—only cared about himself. He'd made that incredibly plain when he left Mom.

Sometimes I wondered why I bothered trying to fit in in a place where I couldn't. Why I tried to blend in at a school full of kids that had seen my face in the papers since they were five years old, thanks to my A-list actress mother and my attorney-to-the-rich-and-famous father. It was a pipe dream that I clung to for irrational reasons.

But I still couldn't let it go.

So I stood against the wall of that party with my cup of skunked beer and pretended to enjoy myself. I drank and drank until my shoulders loosened and a smile spread across my face. I even laughed at some asshat when he got totally shut down by a sorority chick. I had to give it to the girl—she laid a verbal beatdown on him that would have made a lesser man cry. Unfortunately for me, my laughter drew his attention. And the one thing boys hated more than being rebuffed was being humiliated about it.

His narrowed eyes met mine across the undulating crowd, and he stormed toward me, tossing bodies out of his way as he did. I hadn't realized how massive he was until he was towering over me, caging me in against the wall at my back.

"Something funny?"

I put the edge of the cup to my lips and took a long drink. To the casual observer—of which I was certain we had many—it would have looked like one big 'fuck you' to the hulk before me. In reality, it was merely a stalling tactic to buy myself time to think of a way out. Yeah, I could have played the 'do you know who my father is?' card, but I loathed it. Unless it was a matter of life or death, I wouldn't slap that one down on the table.

Maybe not even then.

Eve of Eternal Night

"You hear me talking to you, bitch?"

Ah yes. My favorite word.

I pulled the cup away from my mouth and looked at it for a moment before chucking its contents right in his face. Smart? No. Warranted? Absolutely.

"My name's Eve, not bitch. And I heard you just fine. If your feelings got hurt because I laughed at you, then maybe you should up your game a bit with the ladies. That line was lame as hell."

Anger the likes of which I'd only ever seen in my father's eyes flared in those of the frat boy before me. I don't know if he was drunk or high or crazy as hell, but I watched in slow motion as his hand cocked back to hit me. I focused on the size of his fist as it came flying toward my face. I wondered how much it would hurt when it connected.

It's a reflex to flinch when something comes flying at your face, and that moment was no exception. My eyes slammed shut just before his punch should have landed. When it didn't, I dared to peek through my lashes to see why. Half expecting to find the woman-beater staring down at me with a smile—like he'd just taught me a lesson—I was shocked to find him lying on the ground face down in some questionable fluid.

Looked like someone had taught him one instead.

"I hope I didn't steal your thunder," a male voice said from beside me. I pulled my eyes away from the body on the ground to find a tall, lithe guy standing there, smiling like his life depended on it. The twinkle in his baby blues told me just how much he'd enjoyed what he'd done. I had to give the boy credit—I would not have expected him to lay that guy out without breaking a sweat.

"I was just playing with him," I replied, my eyes drifting

back to the unconscious kid on the floor. "It's more fun to wait until the last second to strike."

The hero's grin grew.

"Couldn't agree more. I think I like your style." His shaggy brown hair hung in his eyes as he bent closer to me. "You got a name?"

"Sure do."

Silence.

His smile widened. "You need another beer?"

"I need one that doesn't taste like rat piss. Can you manage that?"

"Do I get to know your name if I can?"

I rolled his deal around in my mind for a second before agreeing. "Sure."

He winked at me before he disappeared in the crowd, headed toward the back of the house where the kitchen was. For a moment, I wondered if he really didn't know who I was, or if he was just good at playing dumb. I'd fallen for that trick before, and it had ended in a nasty case of blackmail and a whole lot of legal intervention. I'd take a hard pass on that.

I looked toward the front door, wondering if I could make it out before he returned with a drink—possibly roofied to the hilt, with my luck. That was so not the party I was interested in having. With that in mind, I headed through the crowd, wrestling to get through them as they danced and debauched their way into the one a.m. hour. I was almost to the foyer when a gentle hand landed on my arm and turned me around.

Baby blues held up a bottle of imported beer and smiled.

"Gonna need that name now," he said, full of confidence. And in fairness, there was no reason for him not to have it.

He had that boy-next-door charm, with a bad-boy-when-your-daddy-isn't-looking attitude. You could see the mischief in his eyes. It begged to be let out.

"Eve. My name's Eve."

He looked at me strangely, his brow furrowed while he contemplated something. Then realization dawned in his expression, and his mouth went wide. I braced myself for the conversation I knew was coming.

"You teach in the Middleton building, right? You're a chemistry TA?"

So not where I thought that was going.

"Yeah... I am."

"I knew you looked familiar. That long red hair is hard to miss."

With the touch of someone far more intimate with me than he was, he reached for a lock of my hair that lay across my shoulder and drew it between his fingers. He gently caressed one of the waves, a soft smile on his face. He looked like he was in another world—like his mind had gone to some happy place that I totally envied. Nothing had ever made me look so wistful.

Irritated and bitchy were my two defaults.

"And you are?" I asked, pulling away from him until my hair fell from his hand, and his mind returned to the present.

"Sorry." He gave his head a shake, knocking his brown hair into his eyes again. It made him look younger than I assumed he was, and I couldn't help but smile. There was something endearing about him. Something that made me feel safe when it shouldn't have. "My name's Fenris."

"*Fenris?*" I replied in a dubious tone. "That a nickname or something?"

"No."

"Is it your last name?"

His mouth twitched with amusement. "Strike two."

"Are your parents total hippies?"

That one earned me a laugh. "Wrong again. I don't want to hurt your feelings, Eve, but you're a shitty guesser."

"Well then, Fenris, how about you enlighten me. What's up with the name?"

He held out the beer for me to take, and I looked at it with suspicion. "You drink. I'll talk."

"You first," I said, nodding at the bottle.

For the first time since I'd met the curious Fenris, his smile fell away completely. "I didn't mess with it," he said, sounding wounded. "I would never do that."

"Then you won't mind taking a wicked big swig of it, will you?" I leaned closer to him, giving him the same wink he'd given me earlier. "A girl can never be too careful, you know."

"I guess not," he said, putting the bottle to his lips. He looked down the length of it at me with a little heat in his eyes before tipping his head back to do away with half the beer. If he'd roofied it, he was going to black out in no time at all. "Feel better now?"

I grabbed the bottle from his hand and took a drink. "Much."

"Good."

Silence...

More silence...

"So," he said, rubbing the back of his neck. "You go out much?"

I nearly choked on my beer. "I try not to. I find it hard to keep a low profile."

"You famous or something?" he asked, taking the beer from my hand to steal a sip.

"Something like that."

"Or maybe *infamous* is a better description?"

"I think it is, actually."

His smile returned. "I know trouble when I see it."

"So do I." I turned to leave, heading for the front door. I looked back to find him staring at me, his flirty smile gone once again, a rather dark expression in its place. "Thanks for the beer," I said, opening the door and stepping outside. I closed it behind me and rushed down the front steps of the frat house, tossing the beer on the lawn. The bite of the cool night air made me wish I'd worn a long-sleeved shirt, but I made do, wrapping my arms around my waist to keep myself warm.

Walking home alone was something I did often, even though I knew I shouldn't. The campus was relatively safe, but things got a bit dodgy when you wandered off it. That reality had only increased in the last few months. Crime was on the rise—mainly violent ones. Minor road rage incidents had become murders. Muggings were a death sentence. And sexual assaults—well, those didn't end so well either.

With those thoughts rattling around in my mind, I picked up my pace, looking over my shoulder to see if I was being followed. That nagging sensation females seemed to possess was growing stronger with every step. *Danger,* it screamed until I stopped and surveyed the area, searching every dark shadow and shrub for someone lurking—lying in wait. But I found nothing at all. Nothing more than a stray cat in a trashcan and a worn-out flag flapping against one of the brick frat houses.

Maybe I was more intoxicated than I thought.

I took a deep breath before continuing on. Standing in place seemed a shitty plan for staying safe. I was almost through Greek Row to the edge of campus and my apartment that lay a couple of blocks beyond when that feeling again could not be ignored.

Like following a homing beacon, I turned to look down a narrow path between the final two frat houses. The second my mind processed the bloody scene, I took off running, fumbling with my phone as I did, but my fingers were too cold and tight with adrenaline to dial. By the time I reached my apartment, my breath was coming in ragged gasps, and my heart thundered in my chest. I locked the doors behind me for fear I'd been followed and shook my hands until I could successfully call the cops.

I had to tell them about the body.

And the five murderers.

2

I woke up in a cold sweat the next day, wondering if it had all been a dream. My phone was lying next to me in the bed, and I snatched it up, looking for messages from the campus or city police. When I saw none, I scrolled like a madwoman through the local news to see the reports on the crime I'd witnessed. But after five minutes, I didn't find a single one. It was as if it hadn't happened at all.

As if I hadn't seen a dead body between those two frat houses.

"They didn't find it," I said under my breath, dropping my phone to my lap. "How did nobody find it?" Maybe nobody took my call seriously. "Fucking campus police."

It was Friday morning, which meant students would be buzzing around on their way to class. If the dead guy was still there, then someone was bound to find him. Yes, he was tucked away between buildings, but that wasn't enough to keep it secret forever. With that in mind, I threw on a hoodie over last night's clothes and tucked my phone in my pocket. I needed to see with my own eyes that the body was really gone.

Unfortunately, I didn't make it far. Just as I was heading out the door, my phone started buzzing. An unknown campus number flashed on the screen, and I picked it up immediately, wondering if it was the police finally following up.

"Hello?"

"Eve Carmichael?"

"This is she..."

"This is Sarah Medley, from the dean's office..." Oh shit. "He would like to meet with you. *Now*."

Confusion overtook me. "What's this about?"

"The dean will explain when you get here."

She hung up with no further explanation.

I sighed hard, opening the door to my apartment. The dean and I had a rather strained relationship, especially after my father withdrew a sizable donation—a seven-figure one—he'd promised the school. I'd apparently fallen out of the dean's favor after that, not surprisingly. I felt like he'd gone out of his way to make my life miserable from that point on. But he was smart and kept it under the radar.

His office was only about ten minutes away from my apartment, on the other side of campus from Greek Row and the murder I'd witnessed. Thoughts of what I'd seen last night—or thought I'd seen—consumed me as I made my way over to see the dean. Once there, though, I tried to focus on whatever bullshit he was up to.

Sarah looked up from her computer to scowl at me and jerk her head toward the dean's office. I didn't bother acknowledging her in return. I just walked by and opened the dean's door without knocking.

"You called?" I said, the annoyance in my voice plain. Without being offered a seat, I plopped down in the club chair facing his desk and folded my arms across my stomach.

"Ms. Carmichael. There's been a complaint—a report filed with the campus police involving you. I thought it best, given your father's love of retribution, to speak with you directly."

I sat up a little straighter in my chair. Was this about what I'd seen?

"What kind of complaint?"

"Were you at a party last night in Greek Row?"

Yes.

"Why do you ask?"

"Just answer the question, Ms. Carmichael."

"And implicate myself in whatever crime you think I've committed? Without a lawyer present? I think not. Why don't you just tell me what you suspect I've done, and I'll tell you if I did it."

With a dramatic exhale, the dean leaned forward, propping his elbows on his grand mahogany desk. I couldn't help but stare at his thinning grey hair. "You have been accused of knocking out Christopher Martin, the backup quarterback."

I must have gawked at him, blinking repeatedly until a giggle erupted, escaping my lips. Then it grew to a roar of laughter, which, judging by the crease in the dean's brow and the tight set of his features, wasn't appreciated.

"You think I knocked that asshole out?"

"I think that is the complaint he brought to the police. I also think he has witnesses."

"Then those witnesses were drunk or high, because I sure as hell didn't pummel that kid. Don't get me wrong, I wanted to, since he was set to lay me out flat, but I didn't get the pleasure. Someone else stepped in and did it on my behalf."

"And just who was the knight in shining armor that saved you from this alleged attack? The one who knocked Chris unconscious?"

I opened my mouth to say Fenris's name, but nothing came out. Then I slammed it shut. Something deep within me stirred at the thought of giving him up to save my own ass; something dark and wild that balked at being disloyal to the guy that had helped me. No way was I telling the dean his name.

I'd go down for the crime instead.

"I didn't get a name," I said, feigning boredom. "He punched that asshole and I left."

"I find your story rather convenient, Ms. Carmichael."

"That's funny, because I was just thinking that it wasn't convenient at all." I stood up from the worn black leather seat and threw my bag over my shoulder. "Are we done here, *sir?*" I asked, heading toward the door. His answer really didn't matter to me, and we both knew it. His evidence of my involvement in the crime was sketchy at best. It wouldn't hold up in a court of law; of that I was sure.

My dad was an asshole, but he was also the best damn lawyer in New England.

"Not exactly," the dean replied, getting up out of his seat to follow me. "I recently checked in with your academic advisor, and he said he hasn't seen you in over a year." I ground to a halt. "He also said that you're impossible to work with and that he'd be glad to be rid of you when you graduate. While I understand his sentiments and share them, you cannot go without someone advising you your senior year, so I have taken the liberty of setting you up with our newest hire. You're due in his office in fifteen minutes." I turned back to find him staring at me, a smug smile tugging at his lips. "Good luck with that, Ms. Carmichael. You'll need it."

I could hear the dismissal in his tone, so I didn't bother arguing. Instead, I opened the door and left, closing it a little too firmly behind me. The glass pane rattled loudly enough to scare poor Sarah at her desk. I flashed her a smile as I walked past and continued out of the office.

As I made my way to the building's main exit, I considered the dean's words about my new advisor. I hated the idea of having to go there—or do anything he wanted me to, really—but those offices were just on the near side of Greek Row, and I still needed to see for myself if there was any sign of a crime scene where I was sure there'd been one the previous night.

I could drop in quickly to meet my new advisor, make him wish he wasn't, then be on my way. Easy peasy.

With a smile on my face, I strode through the grassy area of campus where kids hung around and studied, killed time, or avoided going to class altogether. The haunting sound of a violin danced through the air, and it almost made me want to stop and listen. Almost. But I had an advisor to torment and a body to find.

I pushed the double doors to the MacMillan administrative building open and took the stairs to the second floor. The halls were empty as I made my way to the main office where the advisors were stationed. One quick inquiry at the front desk and I was ushered back to an unoccupied office and told to wait. Mr. Christensen would be with me momentarily.

Unpacked boxes riddled the room, evidence that he'd

only recently joined the staff. I wondered if one meeting with me would send him running from his contract. The dean had seemed quite confident that I wouldn't be able to walk all over him like I had my last advisor, so I was intrigued. Maybe he was ex-military or something—a real hardass who'd promise to make my life miserable. It seemed likely.

"So," a male voice called out from behind me. "You're the infamous Ms. Carmichael."

I turned in my seat to find the new guy—I assumed—standing in the doorway. He was younger than my last advisor by a solid fifteen years. In fact, he barely looked more than five years my senior. But he held an all-knowing confidence that made him appear older somehow, an arrogance that made me want to shrink down in my seat a bit. And he'd only greeted me.

"I don't know about infamous, but the rest is accurate."

He looked down at the open file in his hands, then back up at me. The unimpressed smirk on his face was duly noted as he walked into the room and sat down across from me at the desk, where I could get a better look at him. Even with his smug look of superiority, I couldn't deny that he was good looking. His clean-cut brown hair was styled to perfection, as was his attire. Not a wrinkle to be seen. For someone working at a school, he had a bit of an edge to his dress clothes, the cut of them tighter than his khaki pant/polo shirt-wearing colleagues. And I spotted the bottom of an intricate tattoo peeking out from his rolled-up sleeve.

As if he'd seen me notice, he tugged his crisp sleeve down to cover it before starting in on me.

"So the word is you're not big on authority, is that true?"

"I think that's fair to say," I replied, settling back in my seat.

"Is it also fair to say that you don't want to be here right now?"

"Yep."

"The dean made you come?"

"Right again."

"And you're just going through the motions?"

"Three for three. You're good, new guy."

"Iver," he said, closing the file he'd placed in front of him. "Not 'new guy'."

"Oh, is this the part where you try to be cool and relatable? I've had therapists try that. It's a total waste of time. I don't relate to anyone."

"I can't imagine why." His droll response hung between us for about a minute before the weight of his pale green-eyed stare started to get to me. Then he floored me with his next remarks. "Your father is an asshole, and you've grown up in the spotlight because of who he is. Your actress mother left, and he screwed her in the divorce, getting sole custody just to stick it to her. You can't trust anyone around you. Your friends have never really been your friends. And every time you think you've found someone you can trust, they betray you, and your armor gets just a little thicker." He pinned me to the chair with his sharp stare. "Sound about right?"

Holy fuck...

"How did you—"

"Just answer the question."

"No," I said, trying to tamp down my rising anger. Yeah, he'd fucking nailed it, and it pissed me off. He stared at me curiously, as though his account couldn't have been flawed. As though that wasn't even a possibility. "You forgot the part about daddy's friends getting handsy whenever he wasn't looking. Otherwise, I'd say you did okay for a dime-store analysis."

"Tell me something, Ms. Carmichael, why are you here?"

"Like in an existential kind of way, or…?"

"I mean, why go to college at all? You clearly don't need to work for a living. I can only assume your father would have provided for you in that regard. Is it the need to appear normal in some way, or is it the desire to have something apart from him? Something he can't dictate and control?"

I didn't bother answering. It was plain in his satisfied expression that he already knew why.

"Let me ask you something, *Iver*. Why are you pretending like you give a flying fuck about who I am or why I do what I do? If you were smart, you'd mark down that I met with you and send me on my way. The sooner you're rid of me, the sooner your life gets easier."

"Maybe I don't want it to. Maybe I like the path of most resistance."

"Then you're in for one hell of a bumpy ride."

He looked down at the manila folder in front of him and cracked it open again, thumbing through the pages until he found the one he wanted. Taking his time, he read through whatever the magical page stated, then looked back up at me, a frown firmly etched on his face.

"When was the last time you saw your therapist?"

"That's none of your fu—"

"*When*, Ms. Carmichael?"

I could feel blood rushing to my face, filling my cheeks with anger. My mental state was none of his business. Neither was my history of therapy.

"I haven't seen the *drug pusher* since I came to this school. Happy?"

"Why did you stop going?"

Because all he did was shove pills down my throat at my father's request.

"Because it wasn't helping."

"Maybe you weren't a good match."

"Maybe I'm broken and there aren't enough meds in the world to fix that."

He continued to stare at me for moment, collecting his thoughts. "I don't think you're broken."

"Well congratulations! You're the only one."

"I'd like you to see someone here on campus. He's new, like me, but I've heard good things. He excels at getting to the bottom of issues and addressing them."

"Sounds awesome," I deadpanned.

"And he's not a psychiatrist, so no meds."

"Just caring and sharing? My favorite."

My eye roll let him in on the secret that it really wasn't, not that he hadn't already put that one together. Ignoring my sarcasm, he reached into his desk and pulled out a business card: Gunnar Fredrickson, Psychologist. The rest of the card was totally blank, except for a campus phone number.

"I think you should call and make an appointment with him. You won't be disappointed."

"I'm sure I will, but I'll let you know."

I got out of my seat, taking the card he offered. It seemed easier to placate him rather than kick up a stink. I could just toss it into the nearest trashcan as I left the building. Iver the all-knowing wouldn't be any the wiser.

But as I held the card in my hand, it seemed hard to discard, even when I hovered next to the garbage on the way out of the main office. Maybe somewhere deep down inside, I knew I needed help. Knew that I couldn't keep up the façade of giving zero fucks forever. It hurt to be hurting and have nobody care—nobody notice. Not even my own father, who lived so close to me but was emotionally miles away, Maybe that's why I actually dialed the number for Gunnar Fredrickson as I walked toward Greek Row.

Maybe I liked the idea of no longer feeling broken.

3

The overly perky receptionist at the student medical center was all too happy to schedule me an appointment with their new therapist. And did I know that I was his first appointment? And this college was so progressive, taking students' mental health seriously!

Clearly she'd had one too many happy pills that morning.

Since my date with Gunnar Frederickson was scheduled and I had no other distractions, I retraced my steps from the night before until I stood on the walkway in front of the narrow divide between frat houses. I knew it was the right one because the rainbow flag that had been ripped down by some bigoted asshole still hung limp from a rope dangling from the third floor window, just like it had the night before.

It was then that it hit me—a wave of fear and nausea that nearly knocked me over. I was more than adept at stuffing my feelings down so deep that they rarely if ever resurfaced, but even I lacked the capacity for denial needed to pretend I hadn't been affected by what I'd seen. Someone had lost their life between those buildings—I just knew it.

I could feel it in my bones.

With careful steps, one after the other, I made my way closer to where I'd seen those five silhouettes standing over the motionless body on the ground. The one that, even in the scant light of the moon, I could see had been covered in blood. There was no way they could have erased every sign of the crime they'd committed. I'd watched enough CSI to know that was impossible. Especially if they were in a hurry.

The buildings seemed to close in around me when I stood where there should have been a body, but wasn't. And there was no sign of blood. I scoured the textured brick exteriors to see if I could find even a single drop of it, but there was nothing. That feeling of nausea rolled in my stomach, but for a different reason this time. This time I wondered if I was losing my mind.

Again.

Iver had been careful not to say my diagnosis out loud when he'd spoken of my previous therapy, but if he'd obtained as much information as it seemed, then there was no way he hadn't seen it. Whatever the technical term for 'breaks with reality' was, that's what I'd had. But only once, right after my parents' divorce when I turned eighteen.

Taking deep breaths, I tried to calm myself. Tried to tell myself that this was different—that I wasn't spiraling down a dark hole. What I could remember of those five days had been the scariest, most empty time of my life, and I'd have given anything not to relive it.

I stumbled backward out from between the buildings and started running across campus toward the med center. My appointment with Gunnar wasn't until later that afternoon, but it was about to get bumped up if I had any say in the matter. I couldn't afford to be swallowed by the darkness again.

Eve of Eternal Night

A SEVERE-LOOKING dark-haired man with harsh, angular features opened the door and poked his head out to spot me waiting in the chair. The corner of his mouth curled up slightly before he waved me in, greeting me warmly.

"Eve, right?"

"That's me. In the flesh. Ready to earn your paycheck, doc?" I asked as he made his way past me into the room.

"I'm not a doctor," he said, correcting me. "Why don't you just call me Gunnar or Mr. Fredrickson? Whichever you're more comfortable with."

"Freddie it is," I replied, leaning back into my third chair of the morning. This one was at least overstuffed and comfortable.

I looked up at him, expecting to find a sour, irritated expression, but I didn't. Instead, a quirked brow and a wry smile stared down at me. He apparently found my behavior amusing.

That was a first.

"Freddie works for me. Now tell me something, Eve. My secretary told me you were adamant about moving up your appointment. Would you like to tell me more about that?"

No.

"I just wanted to get it over with," I lied. Old habits apparently died hard. "My new advisor seemed to have a hard-on about me coming in here. Since I'm already in shit with the dean—for something I didn't do, by the way—I figured I'd comply with the new guy's request. Before someone gets my dad involved."

"Does that happen often?" he asked, sitting down in a chair a respectable distance from me. "People intercede on your behalf?"

I laughed out loud.

"No. Not at all. In fact, my father makes it a point to have as little to do with me as possible; he's too busy with work and his new family. But if it's something nasty that could get tied back to his gleaming reputation, he tends to rush in and threaten lawsuits to shut people up."

I waited for the inevitable 'and how does that make you feel?' When one didn't come, I sat up a little straighter.

"You say your father has little to do with you. Let's explore that a bit."

"There's nothing to explore. It's really quite simple. I'm a reminder of a relationship gone south—the blemish on his perfect record."

"Sounds like a great guy."

I pulled my gaze up from the hole in my jeans I'd been picking at and leveled it on Freddie. He was staring back at me as if assessing my reaction to what he'd said. Maybe that had been his intent, and if so, I'd taken the bait, but I just couldn't tell. There was something in his hazel eyes, a thinly veiled anger that I recognized easily. I'd seen it looking back at me in the mirror more times than I cared to count.

It was then that I really took stock of the man sitting across from me. Though only thirtyish, he had a wizened air about him and a rugged handsomeness that I had somehow overlooked at first glance. And the scar on his left cheek that ran from the lobe of his ear under his cheekbone, stopping just shy of his mouth, was a mystery I suddenly wanted to solve. I had to force myself not to ask him about it.

"Eve?" he asked, as though it wasn't the first time he'd said my name.

"Sorry. What were you saying?"

"I asked if there was another reason that you wanted to

come here today? Something not involving your issues with the dean?"

I stifled my knee-jerk response of 'no' and instead considered telling him what had me so on edge. Telling him what I'd seen the night before—or thought I'd seen. It was risky, knowing that it would likely dredge up my past, which I locked away a long time ago. But for whatever reason, for the first time in as long as I could remember, I felt like I wanted to tell someone my secrets.

Wanted to have someone else share the burden they'd become.

"The last time I told someone about what was really troubling me, I ended up being heavily medicated. That's not a route I want to go down again, Freddie."

"I understand. Is that what you think will happen if you tell me why you're really here?" I let my silence be answer enough. "Like I said, I'm not a doctor so I can't give you any medication. I do, however, have to report you if I think you're a danger to yourself or anyone else." His warm eyes narrowed. "Are you?"

Am I?

"No."

"Then I think you just removed your own roadblock. Would you now like to tell me why you're really here?"

I mirrored his expression, staring back at him with the same intensity.

"I saw something. Last night, after a party. I called the cops, but there was nothing on the news about it today, no rumors spreading across campus. I finally went to the place where I saw it, but there's no evidence that it even took place."

"Maybe you should start by telling me what it is you saw."

"You mean what I *think* I saw."

"No, I mean what you saw. If your mind is so convinced it occurred, then I'm willing to believe it did, if you are."

Freddie was earning points by the second. I took a deep breath and resituated myself in the chair, folding my leg underneath me to sit up a bit taller.

"A murder. I think I saw a murder."

He stilled for a moment.

"Where were you?"

"Greek Row. There was some stupid party there, and I went because sometimes I go just to keep up appearances."

"But you didn't actually want to go?"

"No. I hate those parties."

"So what happened there?"

"What happened there isn't super relevant, but I nearly got laid out by the backup quarterback—that story ties back to me being in shit with the dean, by the way—and some random guy knocked him out and saved the day. He tried to get me to stay and have a beer with him, but I bolted."

"Why didn't you want to stay? Did he do something?"

Freddie sat forward a bit in his chair when he asked that question.

"No, he was fine. Actually, he was funny and kind of sweet, but I don't trust guys like that. It always seems to blow up in my face."

"I'm going to set that conversation aside for now, but we will be addressing your trust issues eventually." Of course. "So you left the party and went where?"

"I walked home. But along the way, between a couple of buildings, I saw these five guys. They were standing around a body."

"Are you sure it was a body?"

"It was a bloody lump of flesh, so yeah, I'm pretty sure it was a body."

"What did you do then?"

"What do you think I did? I bolted for my place and didn't look back. I called the cops, but they either didn't go or somehow didn't find anything when they did, which is why I'm starting to wonder if I saw what I thought I saw."

He sat there quietly assessing what I'd just told him, probably wondering how he was going to delicately break it to me that I was losing it. His silence made me twitchy. I felt like I was going to jump out of my skin. Finally I cracked, jumping up out of the chair and grabbing my bag.

"Forget I said anything," I snapped as I rushed toward the door.

His hand gently grabbed my elbow and pulled me to a halt. It startled me at first, since every therapist I'd ever worked with had made little to no physical contact with me beyond a handshake. When I looked up at his face, I didn't see the schooled, neutral expression I expected. Instead, I saw pain and regret and something else I didn't understand in his eyes.

"Please don't mistake my hesitation for something it wasn't. I wanted to choose my words carefully so that you wouldn't feel like I was manipulating or placating you like others clearly have in the past. I can see that you have a whole history of baggage, and I hope to one day learn about it, Eve. But I have no intention of making you feel like there is something wrong with you. That's the last thing I want."

I tried to muster up a harsh reply, but I couldn't. I was too lost in the thought that maybe, just maybe, Freddie—Gunnar Fredrickson—actually gave a shit about me. That maybe he wanted to help me.

"What if there is something wrong with me?" I said softly, unable to meet his gaze.

"Then we'll fix it."

I tried to quell the hope rising within me, my long history of being disappointed and let down by those around me too ingrained to ignore. But there was something about the look in his eyes and the set of his brow that told me not to abandon the possibility that what had been broken could be fixed. Whatever it was about Gunnar, it made me want to believe him.

Trust him, even.

"I really do need to go," I said, my voice much kinder than it had been. "I'll be late for class."

"We can pick up where we left off on Monday, if possible," he said, releasing my arm. I nodded in response. "I'll have the receptionist call you to schedule."

I didn't dare thank him, afraid my tight throat would betray my emotions, so I just walked away, not bothering to look back. I already knew he was watching me. I'd have done the same if I were him.

By the time I broke through the double doors into the damp outside air, my mind felt clearer, as if just telling someone about what I'd seen last night had purged the fear and confusion I felt about it. A sense of relief washed over me as I walked through the common, pulling my jacket collar tighter around me.

I really did believe that Gunnar would help me.

Maybe my advisor wasn't a complete dick for sending me to him.

4

I stopped to get a coffee on my way to class. Though I wasn't super hung over, I didn't feel amazing, either. My head hurt, and there was an ache in my chest, undoubtedly from stress. Caffeine was needed—in large quantities.

I stopped by the coffee cart and purchased a cup before making my way back out to the common. It was sparsely populated due to the impending rain, but just like earlier that morning, I could hear an eerie tune ringing out through the space, the lone violin still going strong.

I looked down at my watch and sighed. I was already twenty minutes late for organic chemistry. Since there was no easy way to sneak in unnoticed, I wondered if I should bother going at all. Then the violin hit a high note that demanded my attention, and I started walking toward the source as if my feet had made my mind up for me.

On the far side of the knoll, leaning against a massive oak tree, stood the musician whose melodies had called to me. I found a bench a small distance away and sat down to drink my coffee and enjoy the music. I hoped I wasn't overly conspicuous, not wanting to look like a total creeper, but the moment the man behind the music looked over at me and smiled, I knew I'd been busted. Why it bothered me as much as it did, I had no idea.

I held his steel grey gaze for as long as I could before I took out my phone and mindlessly flipped through my emails, hoping to make myself look disinterested. After a couple of minutes, I hazarded a glance up toward him. It was met with an amused grin. He pushed his tall, athletic frame off the tree and started toward me, still playing as he did. Uninvited, he sat down next to me on the bench and continued to play until the song was finished.

Then he just stared.

"Isn't the moisture bad for your instrument?" I asked before taking a sip of coffee. It was so hot that it burned the roof of my mouth, and I winced in pain.

"Careful," he said, still smiling. "Caffeine can be dangerous."

"Clearly."

"And yes, the damp is bad for my violin, but I don't care. Why play something beautiful if you have to stay indoors to do it? Where's the inspiration in that?"

I shrugged, not really knowing what to say. "Well, thanks for the song," I said, getting up. "But I'm late for class."

"Or are you right on time?" he asked, leaning forward a touch so his dark blond hair hung in his eyes.

"Philosophy major, I take it?"

He splayed his arms wide as if to say 'in the flesh'. "I'm a student of life."

"Well, I'm a student of chemistry, and sitting around out here doesn't really help me learn that, so…"

"I feel like there's a line in there somewhere—something

about the chemistry between us—but that would be too easy, wouldn't it? Too childish?"

"It definitely would," I said, collecting my bag from the bench. "You get points for not saying it."

"Would I get points for buying you breakfast to go along with that coffee? Somewhere that doesn't involve a cafeteria or ladies in hairnets?"

I stared at him, doing nothing to hide my dubious expression. He stood there, violin in hand, and waited for my decision. No pressure. No agenda.

"Do you know who I am?" I asked.

"Does anyone really know who anyone else is?" he replied with a grin. When I didn't laugh, he attempted to make himself look serious and tried again. "No. I don't know who you are." Silence. "Do you know who I am?"

"You're the weirdo playing violin by himself in the middle of campus."

"You say 'weirdo', I say 'eccentric man of mystery'."

"If you prefer that..."

He took a step back from me, his grin returning. "I can see that you're not quite ready to let go of your demanding schedule, latte girl, so I will leave you to join the rat race alone." He turned to walk back to his tree and the violin case lying next to it. "Perhaps another time. When you're ready to throw caution to the wind and really *live*."

He didn't look back at me, having politely dared me to go out with him. The open-ended invite was so bizarre that it almost made me want to take him up on it, if for no other reason than to let him know that he didn't have the upper hand in this scenario. But I didn't, of course. I wasn't ready to be *that* kind of headline.

"Hey weirdo!" I called after him. He stopped but didn't

turn around. "You got a name, or should I just refer to you as 'eccentric man of mystery'?"

I saw his shoulders shake with laughter. "I like that, but I prefer Stian. It suits me better."

"Maybe I'll see you around, Stian."

"I'm sure you will, latte girl."

I didn't bother to tell him my name. I liked the idea of him not knowing it. I relished the anonymity.

With coffee in hand, I made my way to class, sneaking in the side entrance when the professor had his back to the class. While he droned on about something that would normally have been of interest to me, my mind wandered over the events of the past twelve hours, trying to sift through all that had occurred.

Then my mind landed on the body in Greek Row and it froze. As if zooming in on the memory like a picture on my phone, it tried to dissect the image, looking for anything to help discern what had really happened last night. Maybe it hadn't really been a murder at all. Maybe it had just been a bunch of guys standing around their buddy who'd hurt himself—possibly knocked himself unconscious somehow. The more I thought about it, the more plausible it seemed. Except for the blood i was sure i'd seen. The blood altogether missing from the scene.

I shook my head, chiding myself under my breath.

I needed to stop watching the news. Immediately. The sensationalized 'journalism' was creating a sense of paranoia in me that I didn't need help with.

As soon as class ended, I spotted Charlie collecting her stuff from the front table. I threw my backpack over my shoulder and made my way over. Charlie was about the only person on campus I considered a friend, but the jury was still out on whether or not she felt the same. She was a bona fide genius. The kind that lacked the social skills to function in the real world. She was going to be a brilliant chemist—probably the one to finally cure cancer or come up with some other award-winning discovery—but she needed to be tucked away in a lab for her own good. People-ing was never going to be her thing.

"Charlie!" I called to her. She turned around and gave an awkward wave.

"You came in late today," she said by way of greeting.

I laughed and shook my head. "Guilty as charged."

She frowned, her full lips pulling down at the corners. "That's not a chargeable offense, Eve."

"And thank God for that!"

She stared at me blankly, most likely trying to sort out how God—if there was one because there was no scientific proof to support religion—had anything to do with it. Her deep brown eyes were pensive, and her brow furrowed as she concocted a response. Her wild black curls were clipped back in an unintendedly asymmetrical way, as though she'd just thrown it in to keep her hair out of her way. All function, no fashion. It was sad, really, because Charlie, under all her nerdy glory, was quite stunning. Her warm brown skin was flawless, and her features were large and well balanced. But nobody ever noticed her beauty. Her general awkwardness and disinterest made it hard.

"So anyway... can I borrow your notes from today and give them back to you later?"

She fished them out of her bag and handed them over.

"I'll be in the lab all afternoon. You can bring them there."

"Perfect. Thanks, Charlie."

"Don't lose them. And don't write on them. And don't give them to anyone else."

"Got it! I won't."

She stared at me for a moment, weighing whether or not she was sold on my reply.

"Why were you late today?"

I let out a sigh. "That's an incredibly loaded question, Charlie. Let's just say my morning started off in the dean's office and went downhill from there."

"Are you on probation or something?"

"Or something. Let's just leave it at that."

"Eve... you'll lose your TA position," she warned, as though I needed the reminder.

"I know. It's all straightened out. No worries."

She stood there silent for a moment before replying. "If you need me to help you, let me know."

I smiled at her. "Thanks. I will." I held up her notes before putting them safely in my bag. "I'll have these back to you in no time. Promise."

"Okay."

With that, she walked out the front exit and disappeared down the hall.

Though she hadn't come right out and said it, she was right; I did need to get my shit together, and thinking about murders that didn't really happen was quite the opposite. I spent the next two hours in the student union, handwriting her notes out to help me learn the material, then studied everything that had been covered so far that semester. After lunch, I studied some more, foregoing my other classes to get caught up. I had been slacking, my apathy for school growing by the day. I couldn't explain why I'd stopped caring. My interest had just seemed to wane slowly as my attention had focused on the growing unease I felt at the shift in the world around me. It made me wonder what the point of it all was if I would just end up shot on my way to class or run over while crossing the street. The more my mind drifted down that path, the emptier I felt. And as the emptiness grew, the more apathetic I became. And so on, and so forth.

I really needed to break the cycle.

It was dark by the time I put my books away, well past dinnertime. I thought about heading home to eat, but instead, I stopped by the lab to give Charlie her notes, then grabbed something from the cafeteria and ate it as I walked home to get my car. It was eight o'clock, which was a perfectly fine hour to go for a drink to celebrate my recommitment to my studies. Nothing says 'getting your shit together' like going for a drink alone, right? Regardless, Friday night cocktails at the Sketchy Fox was a ritual that I intended to keep.

So I got in my car and headed there.

5

Friday night at the Sketchy Fox was usually pretty crowded, but that particular evening, it was packed. I'd barely managed to snag a seat at the bar before the mob stormed in. When I asked Cheryl, the over-the-hill bartender who never skimped on a pour, what was going on, she said they had some new band playing. Apparently said band had one hell of a following. It was downright claustrophobic in there.

I sipped my tequila, leaning my elbow on the bar so I could face the tiny stage at the far end of the place. I loved listening to live music there. Loved blending in with the seedier element that frequented it. Nobody there ever knew who I was, or gave a fuck if they did. It was far from the college scene, which I found refreshing. It was my happy place, where I retreated to when life got a bit too real.

"You need another one, honey?" Cheryl asked, eyeing the guy who had sat down next to me.

"Yeah. That'd be great."

She disappeared behind the bar to retrieve my bottle, then popped back up to set it down in front of me. She

Eve of Eternal Night

didn't ask me for money—she always let me run a tab because she knew I was good for it. Cheryl was about the only person in there that I knew was aware of my identity—or my father's, at least—but she kept that tidbit to herself.

Cheryl was good people.

With a fresh tequila in hand, I turned around in my seat to assess whomever Cheryl had been giving side-eye. I needed to see if moving was in my best interest. But before I could get a good look, someone else bumped into me from behind, knocking me forward into my drink. I managed to catch it before it spilled everywhere, but it took some effort. The guy beside me clearly noticed and had a good chuckle at my expense.

When I tried to wheel around on the asshole that had caused the near miss, I found it difficult to move. His body was too close for me to easily maneuver in my chair, and his hand was planted on the bar, caging me in a bit. Though every alarm in my girl-brain was going off, I looked up to see Cheryl coming over, smiling at the douchebag. And Cheryl never smiled.

"What can I get you, G?" she asked, her tone like honey instead of its normal rasp.

"You know what I like, Cheryl." I could practically hear the wink in his voice as he spoke those words.

She gave a quick reply. I thought I heard her say his name, but I couldn't be sure. Gerrick? Godric? I just couldn't tell; I was too surprised by Cheryl's behavior to pay attention. Knowing she was smitten with him was somewhat comforting, but I was still unnerved by the fact that the old girl had actually flirted with him. He was either an angel among men or one shady sexpot. It was a toss-up really, knowing Cheryl.

I reached over and grabbed his wrist to pry his hand off

the bar and give myself some space. When it didn't even budge, I knew things were about to get interesting.

"Do you mind?" I asked, trying to look over my shoulder at him. Imagine my surprise when I turned my face right into his. Sharp angles and shadows and ice-blue eyes greeted me with an ominous expression. I pressed my body closer to the bar to put some space between us. He laughed in response.

"Don't worry. I don't bite... at least not without asking first."

"Charming," I replied, trying to slither out of my seat and under his arm. My attempt was weak at best, and basically just made me look like I'd fallen off my chair. As I stood in the narrow space between the barstools, Prince Charming's arm still penning me in, I finally got a good look at him.

Cheryl's behavior suddenly made perfect sense.

Everything about him was rugged perfection, from his rocker garb to the five o'clock shadow on his face. Olive skin and short black hair made his eyes stand out even more than I'd originally noticed. And his full lips...

They made it hard to look away.

"See something you like?" he asked, those full lips curling up at one corner.

"I see someone in my way," I replied, but it lacked the bite I'd hoped for. I sounded way too breathy for my own good. Bad boys had been my weakness before everything had gone to shit with my family. Since then, I'd only dabbled in them. At least with a bad boy, I knew what I was getting and could plan accordingly. It was the wolves in sheep's clothing I had a hard time with.

"I see someone who doesn't quite look like she fits in

around here." He made a point to look me up and down slowly before smiling wide.

"Should I get a few more tattoos?" I asked, finally finding my sarcastic tone. I pointed at his neck, where an intricate pattern wound along until it met the stubble on his jaw. "Would that help? Or maybe there's a secret handshake or something I should know...?"

"There's definitely something you should know," he said, leaning his head near my ear. "Unfortunately, I'm more of a show-er than a tell-er." He lingered there for a second while I tried to remember to breathe.

He was upping the ante by the second, and I had no intention of backing down. The fire in my belly—and somewhere a little lower than that—wouldn't let me.

"And when those five minutes are up, then what?" I leaned in, using his tactics on him.

His head dipped low, and the light scratch of his stubble on my ear nearly sent me over the edge. I needed to either jump him or run. There was no in-between. He was the type that dealt only in extremes.

"Then I'd show you again and again and again until you were properly educated."

My breath caught in my throat as I tried to reply. I wondered if that wasn't for the best. My tone would have undoubtedly given away what I was thinking.

The strum of a guitar from the stage broke the tension between us, if only for a second. But it was the second I needed to let my head clear so I could stop thinking with my girly bits. He was trouble for sure, and I needed to remind myself of that.

"Sounds like that's my cue," he said, pulling away from me. Without another word, he pushed off the bar, beer in hand, and made his way through the packed crowd, navigating it with an ease and grace that I wouldn't have thought possible. His swagger as he moved was mesmerizing, and I caught myself staring at him despite my brain's protests. There were bad boys, and then there were guys like him.

He made the bad ones look like angels.

I let out a deep breath and turned back to my drink, slamming it down in one gulp. I made a move to leave, but once the band started to play and the bad boy started to sing, I knew I wasn't going anywhere. I was transfixed. For the next hour, I sat and drank and stared at the lead singer, thinking all kinds of dirty thoughts. The kind you wouldn't even admit to a best friend—even if I had one.

When they took a break, I forced myself to leave. I knew I didn't have the willpower to say no to him, and I didn't want the fallout that would follow hooking up with a guy like him. Fallout would be a definite.

6

The next day, I went to the one place I could always find happiness, no matter what was going on in my life: the local animal shelter a few blocks from school. I volunteered on Saturdays (and Sundays, if they needed me), helping out with whatever they needed. I usually found myself with the newest incomers, especially the badly abused dogs. For whatever reason, I seemed to get through to them over time. I had no problem sitting next to a kennel for hours until the cowering dog inside finally crept its way close enough to sniff me. The dogs deserved to be loved.

And in return, I received the same.

There was something so peaceful about being around the animals. There was no judgment. No expectations (except for belly pats and ear scratches). And they certainly didn't know or care who I was. From the second I set foot in the kennels, all they cared about was the fact that I was there. My presence was enough for them. If I could've rescued them all on my own, I would have.

They were worth their weight in gold.

I walked into the main area and greeted Nancy and Barb, the owners and managers of the facility. They were a pair in life as they were in work, and they were amazing. They, like the animals they cared for, didn't give a shit about who I was.

"Ladies," I said, hanging my coat and purse in the employee room.

"Eve," Barb replied, not looking up from her paperwork. "We've got a new one in the back. A bait dog. Pit bull. I want you to be careful with that one. She's worse than any you've dealt with before."

"Okay. I'll be careful."

"No going in the kennel with her," Nancy added. "Just to be safe."

"Got it."

Without another word, I made my way through the kennel area to the room in the back that housed the newcomers and the dogs that needed to be separated from the main housing area. There, in the final kennel on the left, was a black and white pit bull, scars marring her neck and face. The second I neared the kennel, she backed up, growling, her head low.

"Hey girl," I said, bending down to appear less threatening. "What's your name?" I looked up at the clipboard hanging on the door and saw "Sweet Pea" written in fat print at the top. "Sweet Pea, huh? Is that your name? Sweet Pea?"

Her demeanor didn't change.

"Well, Sweet Pea," I started, sitting down in front of the kennel, "I should probably break this to you gently, but I'm not going to because you're the kind of dog who's been through the wringer, and girls like us need to stick together. Here's the deal: I'm not leaving here until you come sniff me. If you want me to go, you'd better just come over here and do it." I looked up at her, cowering in the corner of her kennel, and smiled. "Guess it's gonna be a long day."

※

Four hours and a sore ass later, I heard the click of nails on concrete coming from inside Sweet Pea's kennel. I didn't want to look up and spook her, so ever so slowly, I slid my hand back toward the chain link and kept my gaze pinned on the far side of the room. Her approach was slow and cautious, and I knew if I made the wrong move, we'd be right back at square one again.

Twenty minutes later, I felt the press of a cold muzzle against my finger. Three sniffs. A snort. Then she ran back into the depths of her kennel. I turned to look at her, sitting with her head a little higher, not a growl to be heard.

"Good girl," I cooed at her softly. I remained seated for a few more minutes before slowly standing up, stretching as I did. I felt like an eighty-year-old. "I'll see you tomorrow, Sweet Pea. Maybe I'll bring you a special treat next time."

I gave her a tiny wave, which made her duck her head, then walked away. It wasn't a breakthrough, but it was progress nonetheless. And with a dog like her, that was huge. I knew what it was like to be her. To be fragile and scared and uncertain. To feel like everyone around you would use or harm you. We were kindred spirits, even if Sweet Pea didn't know it. And as I walked out of the shelter, I vowed to return the next day and pick up where we'd left off. To work hard to help rehabilitate her so that maybe one day she could have the life I strived to.

7

―――――⋖⋘ · · ⋙⋗―――――

Sweet Pea and I had a breakthrough on Sunday after hours of me waiting her out. I'd gone to bed that night ecstatic with our progress. I'd even woken up in a good mood, which was rare for me at the best of times, and lately even more so. I bounced into the kitchen to make coffee and found a buzzkill waiting for me on my phone: a text from Iver, my advisor. It was gruff and to the point. 9:00. My office. So off to his office I went.

"You summoned me?" I flopped down in the chair across from his desk and scowled, letting him know exactly how much I enjoyed being dragged in there on a Monday morning. His angry expression told me how happy he was about it as well.

"I've had a chance to follow up with some of your instructors since we last met," he said, reaching behind his desk to open a drawer. He pulled out the same manila folder and dropped it on his desk. It landed with a loud thwack that grabbed my attention. The file had to be heavy to make that much noise. I leaned forward in my seat, reaching for the file, but Iver snatched it away to open it.

Power move number one.

"Over half of them said your attendance rate is under fifty percent."

"So? I'm still passing."

"For now," he said, looking over at me through his lashes. "Tell me something, Eve. Do you like your TA position in the chemistry department? Like teaching in general?"

"Well I don't do it for the money, that's for damn sure."

He closed the folder and pushed it aside, focusing all his attention on me. The strain in his jaw told me I was getting to him, which made me feel a bit better. Like we were on more even ground. I hated feeling powerless.

"That's not an answer."

"It's an answer, just not the one you wanted."

"Humor me."

I let out a put-upon sigh. "Yes, I like teaching for the chemistry department, okay?"

"Then I have to question why your behavior in your other classes is so reckless. You do realize that if your grades fall, you won't be allowed to TA any longer, don't you?"

"I do enough to keep that from happening."

"You were, but it seems you're dropping dangerously near the point of no longer sustaining that balancing act. Care to tell me why?" I shrugged and sat back in my seat. After a minute of silence, he either got annoyed or realized I wasn't going to answer him. "Here's what I know from your file. I know you're incredibly smart—maybe too smart in some ways—but this attitude of yours... it serves no one but yourself. And I could make an argument that, at this point, it's not even serving you. So why don't you cut the shit and tell me why."

His change in demeanor startled me for a second. He'd

gone from calm and calculated to harsh and aggressive in a heartbeat. I wondered if my advisor didn't have a little pent-up rage of his own that needed to be let out.

I'd have preferred it not be unleashed on me.

"This isn't part of our deal," I said, standing up. I snatched my bag off the floor and started for the door, but Iver was there to stop me. His distance was still respectable, but his presence felt hostile in a way as he loomed above me. "Listen, you sent me to that therapist friend of yours and I went. I'm hashing out my issues with him, which means I won't be doing the same with you. Got it?"

He looked down at me, his jaw working overtime as he reined in his temper. I understood that feeling, the need to tamp down your feelings before they exploded all over those around you, creating irreparable damage. Maybe in some bizarre way, Iver and I had more in common than either of us would want to admit.

And certainly never would.

"Eve," he started, trying to maintain a civil tone, "my job is to ensure that you succeed here—that your future is set on the right course. Do you understand?" Something about the way he said those words niggled at the back of my mind. Like he was talking about my life beyond school, but not. The way his eyes bore into mine only added to that feeling, like he was willing me to see something I couldn't possibly see and had no way to understand, even though he seemed to think I should. "Keeping things from me—shirking your responsibilities—leads to consequences. Far-reaching ones. I can see you don't like me, or any other authority figure for that matter, but that doesn't mean I'm not integral to your success. Don't forget that."

His eyes stayed focused on mine until the weight of them made me squirm. He stepped aside so I could get to

Eve of Eternal Night

the door, and I walked past him, still struggling with that feeling in the back of my mind. The one that said there was something behind his words. Something important.

I all but ran until I was clear of the main office and in the hall. My breath was coming hard as I slowed my pace enough to not draw attention to myself. I pushed open the double doors of the building and stepped out into a storm. Rain pelted my face as I made my way to the student union for food. I couldn't remember the last time I'd eaten. Maybe low blood sugar had clouded my thinking when Iver had said what he'd said.

I grabbed a premade salad out of a cooler and a bottle of juice to go with it, then made my way over to the registers to pay. The same lady that was always sitting there on her swivel stool, playing with her chipped nail polish, rang me up without looking at me and handed me my change.

I looked beyond her into the cafeteria, hating that I'd have to stay there to eat if I didn't want to get more drenched than I already was. But my options were limited, so I cased the room while walking the perimeter, trying to find an inconspicuous spot to sit and eat without disruption. I spotted a table near the back that was being vacated as I approached, and I cut through the middle of the room to get there faster. I'd almost reached my destination when a familiar voice rang out through the room so loudly I wondered if Fenris hadn't used a damn megaphone to achieve that volume.

Not wanting to acknowledge him, I continued as if I hadn't heard my name called. Then I heard it again and knew I was screwed.

"Eve! Wait up!"

The boy clearly wasn't self-conscious. I turned to find him jogging toward me with his food tray in hand. The ridiculous smile on his face made me laugh, but I did my best to stifle it. I didn't want to encourage such displays from him.

I turned away before he reached me and kept walking, though this time I was headed for the rear exit of the building. Getting wet seemed like a better fate than becoming a public spectacle. I knew what that was like. I'd take a hard pass on that any day of the week.

Just as I reached the portal to my escape, a large hand clamped down on the push bar and held it in place. No escaping for me.

"Hey," he said through a wide smile. His eyes practically lit up with excitement, and it made me instantly suspicious. Anyone that keen on seeing me—especially in a public setting—had ulterior motives. At least that had long been my experience. "You in a hurry to get soaked?"

"So it seems."

He looked down at the salad in my hand, then back at me.

"Why don't you eat that here? I'll keep you company."

"I'm not so great with company," I said, holding his gaze. "I'm kind of a loner, if you hadn't figured that one out yet."

His smile widened. "I'm starting to."

"Clever boy."

"Does this go back to your whole 'a girl can never be too careful' schtick? Because I'm pretty sure we're in an extremely crowded room full of smartphone-wielding students. The risk factor seems pretty low."

"Then I guess you haven't seen what kind of damage those iPhone-wielding students can do," I said, leaning against the push bar on the door. His grip on it still held, but his smile did not. It faded away slowly, leaving a look of concern in its wake.

"Eve—"

"I just need to get to class, that's all. It's nothing against you. Promise."

He didn't seem fully satisfied with my response, but he released the bar regardless, allowing me to leave.

"You're breaking my heart," he said, forcing a smile that never quite reached his eyes.

"I don't have one, so I can't relate. I'll see you around."

He gave a little wave as the door closed on him. I could feel him watching me disappear into the veil of rain that seemed to fall harder with every step I took. I was soon running toward the chem building, trying to figure out why a part of me wanted to run back to Fenris.

8

―――▄◄◄··▶▶▄―――

"Eve!" Fenris shouted from down the hall as I exited the class I TA'd. I could hear his heavy footfalls echoing off the cinderblock walls as he ran to catch up. I stifled a laugh so that my stone face would be in effect when he finally caught up. "Wait up!" I pretended I didn't hear him and just kept walking. Just as I'd expected, he continued his pursuit until he jumped in front of me, looking disheveled from his dash down the hall. "Jesus, you walk really fast."

"I walk with *purpose*," I corrected. "As every girl should."

"Can't be too careful," he said.

"No, Fenris, you sure can't."

"Ha!" he shouted before realizing just how enthusiastic he'd sounded and lowered his voice. "So you remember my name."

"Well, in fairness, it's kind of hard to forget," I said, continuing on to my tiny TA office.

"I'm kind of hard to forget," he countered with a smile.

"That's one way to put it. Now if you'll excuse me, I have

office hours in a bit, and I need to get a few things done before that."

"I know you have hours. That's where I'm headed."

I stopped and shot him a dubious look. One that he clearly found amusing.

"You need help with your homework, do you?"

"Yep. Sure do."

"Why do I find that hard to believe," I mumbled to myself as I walked past him.

"I also have something else I want to ask you about, but I'd rather not do it out here."

That got my attention. I looked at him over my shoulder, trying to see if I could learn anything from his expression, but he gave nothing away.

"Fine. Follow me."

Like a good little pup, he walked at my side with his mouth closed until we reached my office. I unlocked it and opened the door, flipping on the light switch as I stepped in. Fenris closed the door behind him and stood in front of it as if on guard.

"It's about what happened the other night," he said, hovering in a way that started to make me nervous.

"Did the dean find out it was you that knocked that kid out?" I asked, assuming that's what it was. "Because I didn't tell him anything when he grilled me. I said I hadn't seen whoever dropped the wannabe quarterback."

Fenris looked at me with confusion in his eyes for a moment until realization dawned in them. He quirked a brow as he folded his arms across his chest. It was then that I knew he wasn't there to discuss his knockout punch.

Dammit...

"So the dean called you in about that incident? He

wanted to know who did it and you didn't tell him it was me?"

"He actually brought me down there to accuse me of doing it, but—"

"You didn't tell him because you didn't want me to get in trouble."

The boy couldn't have looked more pleased if he'd tried.

"I didn't tell him because I hate him with the fire of a thousand suns and would never give him any help intentionally. Also, I don't know your last name."

He made a face at me that screamed 'nice try' and took a step deeper into the room. "I'm pretty sure this school isn't crawling with students named Fenris. I think my first name would have sufficed."

I shrugged, not wanting to get into it because the truth was, I didn't fully understand why I hadn't turned him in. It would have gotten the dean off my back—a benefit not easily outweighed. But for some reason I couldn't explain to myself, let alone the eager-looking guy standing before me, the idea of handing him over for his crime had just felt wrong. Whether it was because he'd done it to protect me, or some other reason, I didn't know. All I knew was, the thought of it felt like a betrayal.

"You want to know why I think you didn't do it?" he asked, taking another step closer.

"Not really—"

"I think you like me."

"I like that you knocked a guy out for me."

He shook his head. "I think you actually *like* me, regardless of my right cross. I think you didn't want to bail on the party that night—that you really wanted to stay and get to know me."

"And by get to know you, you mean sleep with you?"

His approach came to a grinding halt. "No. No, I don't." He looked at me with a hint of sadness in his eyes, and it was so earnest and so honest that I had to look away from him. "Eve," he said, taking cautious steps toward me. "Whatever you think I had planned for you that night, I didn't. I just wanted to talk to you. To be around you. That's all."

I shuffled some papers on my desk. "Yeah, well, you'll have to excuse my skepticism. It's served me well for a really long time, and it's a hard habit to break."

His hand closed gently over mine, stopping me from my unnecessary stacking of tests to be graded.

"Eve, please look at me." With a harsh exhale, I did just that. "I'm sorry for whatever's been done to you to make you feel like you need body armor just to get through the day, but you don't need it with me. I'm not that guy."

And that's where you're wrong, Fenris...

"We might have to agree to disagree on that one."

"Let me prove it to you," he said, dipping his head lower so he could look into my eyes.

"I'm honestly frightened by what you're about to say."

"Go out with me. Just dinner. A highly public place of your choosing. I'll even meet you there if you don't want me to drive."

"Fenris, I can't—"

"You *can*, Eve. All you have to say is 'yes, Fenris, that sounds amazing'."

"But if you've come here today for help with chemistry, then you're technically my student."

He threw his arms up like he was celebrating something. "See! That makes it even better. It's frowned upon. And you seem like the kind of girl who loves to do what she isn't supposed to."

Damn, he had me on that one. "Okay, Fenris, answer me

this. If I say yes to this date—which I'm not saying I am—what are the odds of you leaving me alone after that?"

"Slim to none," he replied, totally deadpan.

"Fuuuuuuck," I said, dropping into my chair. "Is this your plan? Just wear me down until I have to date you?"

He shrugged. "I mean... if it works..." Before I started to go off on him, he smiled, letting me know he'd totally played me. "Girl, you need to calm down before you blow a gasket or something."

"I have no idea what that means, but it sounds messy."

"It's very messy. You should probably avoid it by giving me what I want so I'll leave and let you get to work."

I stared up at him for a long moment, wondering what exactly I was going to do with this stray pup that had latched onto me.

"Have you no shame?" I asked, choking on a laugh as I said it. I would stew about my inability to stifle it for the rest of the day. The second my façade broke, he knew he had me. I was going to go out with him against my better judgment. Fenris had won.

And I'd finally met someone more stubborn than I was.

"Does that mean yes?" he asked, smiling down at me like a boy up to no good.

"Ugggggh, yes. It means yes. Now get out of my office before I call campus security and have you removed."

"Am I picking you up?"

"Do you know where I live?"

That damn smile got wider and more mischievous. "Not yet. But I'll be over at eight."

"Make it six. I plan on being home early."

That comment earned me a laugh. "I'll be there at seven, and we'll see how it goes."

"Spoiler alert: it ends with me at home watching a movie alone and you having a cold shower."

More laughter. "See you at seven." He strolled out of the room like a man who'd just done the impossible, then closed the door behind him. For the next two hours, I stared at the clock on my computer and wondered how Fenris the Great had managed to trick me into going out with him.

I hadn't been on a date in years.

But I had one in five hours.

9

At five minutes of seven, there was a knock on my apartment door. My hope that Fenris wasn't nearly as crafty as he thought was dashed in an instant. He'd not only ascertained where I lived, but also managed to finagle his way into the building without buzzing me. Like it or not, I really was about to go on a date with him.

In reality, it wasn't the worst thing to happen to me. He was tall and good-looking and funny. At minimum, the evening would prove entertaining, and I needed a little more humor in my life. My concern started to creep in when I thought about the after-date stuff. The awkward lingering. The asking to come up to my room. Yeah, I had no problem shooting him down and wounding his red-blooded male pride; the problem was whether I'd want to or not.

I took a deep breath and tried to think of all the ways I could push him away before I took leave of my senses and let him in. Letting that happen was undoubtedly my worst-case scenario and one I couldn't allow, no matter how cute he was when he turned that devilish smile on me.

Eve of Eternal Night

A second knock on the door, followed up with "I know you're in there" from my date, brought me back to the present.

"Coming!" I yelled, turning off the TV and prying myself off the couch. I walked over to the door and opened it to find Fenris standing there wearing that shit-eating grin. A part of me wanted to slap it off his face.

Another wanted to do something else entirely with it.

I quickly looked away in search of my boots. He stepped inside my place and closed the door.

"Leave it open," I said quickly. There was an obvious note of panic in my voice that I couldn't take back. All I could do was hope that Fenris hadn't heard it, but one look at his face and I knew he had. Concern furrowed his brow. "I'm sorry. I didn't mean to snap at you. It's just... we're about to walk out anyway..."

Weak. Totally weak excuse.

"Sure," he said, forcing a smile at me. I'm sure it was meant to fluff over the whole thing, but it lacked the normal spunk I expected, so it made things worse. He clearly knew something was wrong.

"So," I said, slipping on my boot. "Where are you taking me?"

"That makes it sound like this is a kidnapping... or a hostage situation."

Wasn't it?

"I'm not leaving here until I know where we're going." The firm set of my hands on my hips told him I meant business. He shook his head and laughed.

"Dinner. We're going to dinner. Is eating acceptable to you, or are you a breatharian or something?"

"I literally have no clue what that is, so no, I'm not that."

"It's this group of people who don't eat. They just live off the energy of the air and—"

"Okay, let's go," I said, pushing him through the door before he could go into a long-winded explanation of something I didn't care about. We had all of dinner for that to happen.

He led the way down the stairs to the first floor and out to his car parked in front of the building. I was surprised by the make and model of it. I hadn't pegged him for a high-end SUV kind of guy; I'd expected more of a daddy's-hand-me-down to be waiting for me. It made me wonder about who Fenris really was, and whether maybe he and I had more in common than I would have thought.

"You ready?" he asked, opening the passenger door for me.

"Such a gentleman." He made a small gesture with his hand before bowing.

"I think you'll find I'm full of surprises once you get to know me."

"White knight syndrome?" I asked, standing inside the car door looking up at him.

He simply shrugged in response. "What can I say? I'm old fashioned."

"We'll see about that," I mumbled under my breath as I climbed in.

Damn if that didn't turn out to be true.

૭૦

"You eat a lot," I said, watching him carve up the massive porterhouse steak he'd ordered.

His mouth curled up at the corner around his cheek full of food. "I'm a growing boy."

"Pretty sure guys stop growing at twenty-one. Tell me you're not younger than that. Please. I can't go out with someone unable to order a drink at a bar."

His smirk grew to a smile. "So you want to go out with me, huh? Movin' a little fast for someone who put up such a stink about having dinner with me."

"You know what I meant."

"Do I?" he asked, his eyes alight with mischief.

"I meant that I can't be the only one drinking tonight. And I will be needing alcohol… lots of it."

He looked at me, still smiling, and flagged the waiter over. To prove his age, he ordered a beer (after showing his ID), then turned his gaze to me.

"Your turn. And remember to pick wisely. You always want to end with what you started the night drinking."

A challenge, loud and clear. "I'll have a shot of tequila."

The waiter looked at me strangely, then double-checked that he'd heard me correctly. When he seemed satisfied, he turned and walked away. Fenris met my obstinate stare with wide eyes.

"I gotta say, Eve, I like your style."

When the waiter returned, I accepted the tumbler of amber liquid and tossed it back with one gulp, placing the empty glass back down on the table. I smiled at Fenris, inviting any other challenges he might have for me with that look. It said 'bring it' as plain as day. He made a show of taking another bite of steak and chewing it slowly, as if to say 'girl, I've got all night'.

Try though I did, I couldn't subdue my amusement with his antics. I smiled despite myself, then quickly looked down at my plate, taking an interest in my pasta.

"Why do you always shy away when you smile?" he

asked, his tone suddenly serious. I kept my eyes down and pushed a piece of penne around my plate with my fork.

"I don't know... I guess it makes me uncomfortable."

I dared a glance up at him through my lashes. The tight set of his features surprised me. For someone who didn't seem to take things too seriously, he sure as hell looked serious about that. He opened his mouth to say something, then snapped it shut. A moment later, he tried again.

"Happy looks good on you," was his response before he turned his attention back to the half-cow on his plate.

The sharp retort I'd prepared fell limp on my tongue. "Thanks," I said quietly, hating how small I felt when I said it. Something about that boy made me feel soft—vulnerable—and I both loved and hated it. Soft only led to pain, a lesson I'd learned a long time ago. Letting people in only ever ended one way—badly.

I tried to muster my armor to ward off his charms, but my heart seemed reluctant to fully suit up. It was determined to leave a spot exposed for Fenris to claim. And my brain couldn't dissuade it. In short, I needed to get away from Fenris as fast as possible before I did something stupid, like let him in.

But that didn't happen.

And my inaction had consequences.

10

—◄◄⟨·•·⟩►►—

By the time we left the restaurant, the two shots of tequila had kicked in. I laughed wildly at some ridiculous story Fenris was relaying—something about a dare and mooning a cafeteria full of students and getting chased out by the lunch lady with a wooden spoon. His ability to reenact it was uncanny; I felt like I was there with him. Tears streamed down my face as I clutched my stomach, contracted to the point of pain because I was laughing so hard. Fenris was only fueled by my reaction, and he kept it up until I begged him to stop. I braced myself against the brick façade of a building, doing all I could to slow my breathing and stop snorting. It wasn't an attractive sound, but I couldn't help it. I always did it when I laughed that hard.

I hadn't done it in so long, I'd almost forgotten.

"Please!" I begged between gasps. "I'm going to pee my pants!"

"She only got one good whack in," he said, totally ignoring my pleas. Though I was turned so I couldn't see his face, I could hear in his tone how much he was enjoying torturing me.

"Fenris, so help me God, if I urinate in the street because of you, I promise this will be our first and final date!"

He fell quiet in an instant.

I took that moment to get control of my breathing as well as my bladder. Once I felt certain I wasn't going to have an epic accident, I turned to find him smiling down at me. For the second time since I'd met Fenris, he knew he'd won.

And it was really starting to get on my nerves.

"Payback is hell, mister. That's all I'm gonna say."

"I await it with bated breath."

He reached a hand out toward me—such a casual gesture, but one that seemed to mean so much more in that moment. I looked at it as though how I proceeded could forever alter the course of my life. Had I known then that it would, I wondered if I would have taken it. But in that moment, with the pale light of the moon reflected in his blue eyes as they stared back at me full of hope and need, it felt so right to extend my hand toward his and accept what he offered. The second we touched, a sense of safety washed over me unlike anything I'd ever felt before. It warmed me in places I'd never realized were cold. Frozen, even.

It awakened a part of me that would never go back to sleep.

FENRIS INSISTED on walking me to my apartment building from the car, using my famed 'can never be too careful' line against me. I was starting to regret having ever said that in front of him. He parroted it whenever it suited his purposes.

Clever little bastard.

"Do you want me to walk you up?" he asked as we stood in front of the main entrance.

"Are you afraid I'm going to be jumped between here and the third floor?"

"It happens."

"And then what? Are you going to offer to escort me from my living room to my bedroom? Just in case?"

His eyes went from playful to full of lust at the mere mention of my bedroom. Clearly I hadn't fully thought that comeback through. My cheeks flushed as my heart started to race. Seeing how flustered I was, he leaned in toward me, his pace slow but sure. Those bright blue eyes held my gaze as he bent his head down toward mine, leaning in for a kiss.

"I should go!" I blurted out, fumbling with my keys to open the exterior door.

I heard him chuckle before exhaling hard. "Aren't you supposed to have those out and ready to go when you come home at night?"

"Why? Aren't you here to keep me safe? I thought that was the point."

He went quiet for a moment, and I looked up over my shoulder to find sharp eyes looking down at me.

"I will always keep you safe," he replied. His words carried a weight that settled on my heart, slowing it considerably. I had no idea how to reply to that, so I forced a smile, then turned to unlock the door. Once it was open, I stepped halfway through and looked back at the funny-yet-serious boy standing behind me.

"I had fun tonight," I said.

"Maybe you'll let yourself have fun another night... with me."

"Maybe," I replied, letting a genuine grin escape.

It earned me one in return. "Give me your phone," he

said, reaching his hand out for it. I did, then watched as he punched his name and number into my contacts. "There. Just in case you need it." He handed the phone back to me before starting down the steps. "I'll see you around, Eve."

"You will."

As the color started to return to my cheeks, I turned away from Fenris and walked into the foyer of my building, letting the door fall shut behind me. I climbed the stairs, not looking back to see if he was still standing on the steps watching me through the window in the door. He'd been so concerned about my safety that I just assumed he was.

His chivalrous nature was endearing.

I was still smiling about our date when I reached my floor. I sent him a quick text to wish him good night. Two seconds later, I received one with the same sentiment from him.

I unlocked my apartment door to find it brightly lit, just as I'd left it. I always kept the lights on when I knew I'd be coming home late. It made me feel better to walk into a semi-lit room rather than one shrouded in darkness. The dark had always left me a little unsettled, from the time I was a child into adulthood. My imagination was almost impossible to rein in.

I tossed my keys onto the kitchen counter and put my purse down beside them. Having forgotten to lock the door behind me, I rushed over to it and latched the deadbolt as well as the chain. Had there been a third option, I'd have locked it, too. The increasing crime in our area was always fresh in my mind. I didn't want to become the next headline.

Once the door was secure, I headed into the bathroom to get cleaned up for bed. I studied myself in the mirror as I took off my makeup, turning my face to catch the harsh vanity lighting. Even without an ounce of makeup on, I was attractive. My creamy complexion paired with my green eyes and red hair was eye-catching. The smattering of freckles across the bridge of my nose that spread onto my cheeks before thinning out used to be the bane of my existence, but with age I'd grown to like them. I ran my finger over them as if to smooth them out. I wondered if Fenris had noticed them—if he'd wanted to touch them as I was.

My fingers slid down to my lips, tracing over them lightly. I wondered what Fenris would have done to them if I hadn't run away. My eyes rolled closed at the thought of his lips brushing mine—a light graze of his teeth against my bottom lip before he captured it and tugged on it, toeing the line between pleasure and pain. My breath caught in my throat before I exhaled hard, forcing my eyes open. Pink, flushed cheeks greeted me in the mirror, taunting me. No amount of denial could cover up the fact that I wanted Fenris to kiss me. Possibly more.

Trying to clear that thought from my mind, I finished washing my face and brushing my teeth before I walked down the tiny hall to my bedroom. I checked to make sure the windows were locked—even though I was on the third floor—and the blinds were down. I reached over my nightstand to close the blind on the final window, but something outside caught my eye. I bent down low to avoid being seen, even though the light in my room was off.

Below, amid a small patch of bushes and trees near the building, a shadow loomed by the trunk of an old oak that stood tall in the middle of the landscaping. I squinted hard, trying to make out what was tree and what was shadow, but it was difficult with so little light falling on that part of the property. I held my breath as I willed the darkness to move. Moments later, the shadow leaned forward just enough to show a human silhouette. I shot up onto my feet, running to the kitchen to grab my phone. I dialed Fenris as I ran back to my room, adrenaline surging through my veins.

"Eve?"

"There's someone outside, hiding in the bushes by my apartment."

"Don't move, understand? I'll be right there."

"Shit!" I cursed, straining to see if the figure was still there. I'd only been gone for ten seconds at most. Had he seen me jump up in the window? Had I scared him off?

"What?" he asked, his voice low and commanding.

"I can't see him now... I think he's gone."

"I'm coming over—"

"No. No, it's okay. I think I just spooked myself."

"Eve," he said, his tone still serious. "I'm coming over."

"Honestly, Fenris, I'm fine. I'm sorry I freaked out and called."

"You can always call me, Eve. *Always*. For anything."

I hesitated for a second before responding. "Why? Why are you so intense about that, Fenris?"

Silence...

"The world is a scary, uncertain place. I want you to know you have someone to turn to when you need one. Someone who has your back."

"But you barely know me."

Another pause.

"I do know you, Eve. Better than you can imagine."

"Did my father hire you?" I asked, my normal skepticism taking over. "Did he send you here to keep me safe?"

"No," he said, sounding confused and hurt. "I have no idea who your father even is."

"Then how can you know me?"

"Because I see you, Eve. I see the hurt and the doubt and the fear peeking out from under that armor you wear. I know you're more than what's been left in the wake of whatever's hurt you."

"I—" I cut myself off before I let my guard down. It was easy to want to do that with Fenris. It was easy to be lulled into a false sense of security. Though I wanted to tell him that he was right—that I had built my tough-girl façade on the hurt of my past, that I'd been damaged by my years in the spotlight—I couldn't. Partly because I wasn't ready; but mostly because I didn't want Fenris to prove me right. That he, too, was just another person trying to use me in one way or another. "I'm sorry I bothered you, Fenris. Good night."

I hung up the phone before he could protest and laid it down on the nightstand next to my bed. For the next few minutes, I stared out at the darkness below and wondered if I had really seen the shadow move, or if it had been fatigue and tequila and my overactive imagination at work. I really needed to stop obsessing over the news so much. It did nothing for my state of mind. Crime wasn't exactly around every corner. Unless it was.

Especially around the corner of a Greek Row building, where a body had lain lifeless and murderers had loomed.

With that memory dredged up, I crawled into bed and tucked my phone in next to me. I lay there for hours, hoping sleep would eventually take me and quiet my mind, but it didn't. Sleep was as evasive as the answers surrounding the murder that wasn't. The crime that had never happened.

At five in the morning, I got up and called the student med center.

I needed to meet with Gunnar ASAP.

11

———⟪⟨⟨ · • · ⟩⟩⟫———

I hadn't yet heard back from Gunnar's secretary when I made my way to campus. I was tempted to stop in and wait to be seen, but I had class. Begrudgingly, I made my way through the common to the astronomy building.

Along the way, distraction found me.

"Well, well, well... look who it is. Latte girl strikes again." Stian's steel-grey eyes looked up from his book as I approached, and he smiled at me. It promised mischief and shenanigans and everything in between. "Where is your namesake? Have you suddenly deserted your favorite beverage?"

"I had one at home," I said, hovering above him. Taking the hint, he dog-eared his page and closed the book before unfurling his body to his full height. He seemed taller than I remembered. Taller and slightly more imposing.

"Heading to class?"

"Unfortunately."

"I wonder what your parents would think of your disregard for your education."

Eve of Eternal Night

"They probably couldn't give two shits less. Besides, it's a fluff class. It doesn't really have any impact on my major."

"Fluff class, she says. I wonder what it could be. Creative writing? Statistics? ... Philosophy?"

"Astronomy, actually."

That devilish grin returned. "That might not impact your major, but it certainly impacts your *life*. You should go—actually, we both should." He reached out his hand for mine, and I hesitated. "It's just a hand. The gesture only means as much as the weight you give it." I stared at it for a beat before slowly extending mine toward him. His smile returned the second he took my hand in his.

Then we were off toward the Stewart-Thompson science building.

"Which room?" he asked over his shoulder.

"205."

"Perfect. We can sneak in the back."

"You're really going to go to a class that you're not even enrolled in?"

He shrugged, still holding my hand captive. The fact that I'd let him have it in the first place still surprised me. But there was something warm and soothing about his skin against mine—a feeling I didn't want to lose—so it stayed where it was.

"I'm a student of life, and the stars are my guide. I'm offended by your indifference. I think I need to give you an off-curriculum education in them."

"So you're just going to whisper in my ear all class while the professor is talking?"

He looked back at me, his eyes sparkling with the thrill of doing something he knew he shouldn't. "Exactly."

"You're crazy!" I said, feeling the rush of adrenaline in

my veins. It was surprisingly welcome. "We're going to get in so much trouble."

"If by trouble you mean that the professor might not care for our sidebar conversation and throw us out, then yes, we likely will."

His lack of concern over getting tossed from class floored me.

"All right. I'll do it, but I swear on all that's holy, if we get kicked out and the dean catches wind of it, I'm throwing your ass under the bus and saying you kidnapped me at gunpoint and made me go with you."

"Duly noted," he said, pushing open the door to the building. With my hand still hostage in his, we climbed the stairs to the second floor. I couldn't decide if he thought I was going to make a break for it if he let me go or if he was just the touchy sort, but in either case, I found him darkly amusing, so I let him have his way.

He stopped at the rear entrance to the auditorium-style classroom, giving me one last chance to bail on his little mission. The challenge in his eyes as he stared at me was enough to make me follow through. I didn't back down from much—not if I could help it. Backing down from his stunt wasn't going to happen. Period.

He eased the door open and walked down the narrow passage leading to the back row. Because the seating was higher there, we could still be seen sneaking in, but thankfully the lights had been dimmed so the class could see the pictures on the projection screen.

"If you look up at the right corner of this picture, you can see the point of Aquarius and follow it down," said the professor whose name I'd never bothered to learn, pushing his thick glasses up onto the bridge of his nose.

"He's going over the zodiac signs," Stian said softly in my ear. "And you thought this lecture wasn't important."

He pulled away to flash a toothy grin at me in the darkness. The guy sitting directly in front of us turned a nasty glare our way, and I gave him one in return.

"What did you expect sitting in the back row?" I said to him. He muttered something about me buying my way through school as he turned around. I gave the back of his chair a boot, knocking him forward. Seconds later, he slid down a few seats in his row.

Good call, kid. Good call.

"You have quite a way with people," Stian mused in my ear.

"Generally speaking, I can't stand them."

"If I actually valued another's opinion of me, I might be wounded by such a statement."

"I'm here, aren't I?"

"True! Now the professor is going to go into all the technical jargon regarding this particular constellation, which is boring as all hell. I'm going to give you a little history on Aquarius instead. The *actual* history, and not some psychic-flunky's version of it."

When I didn't reply immediately, he stuck his face in mine to read my reaction.

"Great! Prattle on about the stars in three... two..."

He flashed me a mildly irritated face before settling back in his chair, leaning close to speak into my ear.

"It's been long said throughout history that all the zodiac constellations are more than just conglomerations of stars in the sky—that they have a purpose far beyond that. The great astronomers have theorized over centuries about how and why they came to be. Some believed that the gods put them there for navigating the Earth. Others told tales of wronged lovers and punished soldiers and myriad other stories that could explain the likenesses in the sky. But there was never really a way to prove why they existed."

I nestled back into my seat and let the wistful, faraway sound of his voice lull me. There was something so wild but peaceful about Stian—something that spoke to a place deep inside of me. Even the tenor of his voice seemed to put me at ease.

"Why do you think Aquarius is up there?" I whispered.

"I like to think it's a portal to another dimension."

I turned to him, laughing a little under my breath.

"Of course you do. Are you hoping to be beamed up there one day, Scotty?"

He didn't turn to look at me. Didn't flash me a wry smile or an admonishing glare. Instead, he just stared at the screen in the front of the room with a reverence in his eyes that I couldn't understand but had to appreciate.

"Yes. I am."

"But... how? How could you live in the stars, even if it were possible? You'd die!"

It was then that he turned to face me, that same faraway, reverent look in his eyes. "Would that bother you? To know that my soul had gone somewhere else?"

"Ummm..." I said, clearly stalling. I had no clue what to say to that. I'd only just met him; I hadn't exactly put a lot of thought into what life would be like if he disappeared into the stars the next day. But when I did contemplate it, I realized that the answer was yes. It would bother me. "Are you planning on leaving tomorrow?" I asked, trying to lighten the mood that had grown so heavy in a flash.

He took the bait and smiled back at me. "Depends on your answer."

"You're so odd—"

"Your answer?"

"Yes, it would bother me, okay? Weirdo..."

I choked on a laugh, then shrank down further in my seat as the professor turned his attention to the students in the room, searching for the disruption. I was surprised that the guy that had moved didn't serve me up on a platter.

Stian's teeth gleamed in the scant light as he smiled at me, clearly feeling like he'd just won a battle I hadn't realized we were fighting.

"Then I guess I'll stay."

He leaned back and laced his hands behind his head. I took that opportunity to backhand him in the stomach. He lurched forward, exhaling hard, and I had to cover my mouth to capture the laughter that threatened to escape. He looked hilarious—the shock in his eyes was plain. Then those eyes narrowed on me, and I knew I was in trouble.

I snatched up my bag and bolted out of our row, headed for the back door. I could feel him racing after me, but I didn't care. I just wanted to make it to the hallway so I could break down in hysterics.

About ten feet from the classroom, I collapsed against the wall, clutching my stomach as I laughed until I cried for the second time in days.

"Your face..." I said, gasping for breath. "You should have seen your face."

"I take it you didn't want to stick around to learn about Gemini next?"

His deadpan response only fueled my outburst.

When I calmed down enough to stand up straight, I wiped the tears from my eyes on my sleeve. A couple deep breaths later, I was a solid seventy-five percent under control. I just hoped he didn't say something else funny. I wouldn't have been able to handle it.

"I think I'm good with learning today," I said, my voice still a bit strained.

"How about that breakfast you turned down the other day, then? Does that fit into your schedule? I'll tell you all about Gemini while you eat some gluten-free bagel with dairy-free cream cheese on it."

"Is that even a thing?" I asked, wondering what dairy-free cream cheese would even be made of.

"It's not, thank the gods." He shuddered for good measure, letting his loathing for dairy tampering be known. "What do you say, latte girl. You in?"

"I'm in, but I pick the place."

"Ah," he said, feigning surprise. "A creature of habit, I see. No more throwing caution to the wind?"

That sparkle in his eyes flared, challenging me to live in the moment. The problem was that niggling sensation in the back of my mind reminding me that I didn't know him —like at all—other than the fact that he liked to loiter in the common, sneak into classes he wasn't taking, and wanted to escape our dimension through a portal in Aquarius. To argue that he was of completely sound mind would have been a stretch, even for my father. But still... there was a freedom to being with him that made me want to follow him like the Pied Piper, even if it seemed a dodgy idea.

"Fuck caution," I said, picking up my bag. "Where are we going?"

"Not far," he said, leading the way to the stairwell. "And I promise I'll bring you back. In one piece, even."

"How considerate of you."

"What can I say?" he replied, splaying his hands wide in a placating gesture. "I respect the natural order of things."

We stepped outside into the cool morning air, and he continued toward the far side of campus. As I followed him, my phone started vibrating in my pocket. I pulled it out to see that the med center was calling.

"Hold up!" I called after him, and he stopped. I clicked 'talk' on my phone and put it to my ear. Gunnar's secretary informed me that he had time if I could come straight over. If not, he didn't have anything available for the rest of the day. "I'll be right over. Thanks." Then I hung up.

"Somewhere you suddenly have to be?" Stian asked, his gaze sharper than usual.

"Yeah. I have an appointment I can't miss. Rain check?"

His eyes softened and he smiled.

"For latte girl? Always."

"Sounds good. Thanks for the lesson today. It was fun."

"Just wait until I tell you all about Gemini."

Without another word, he turned and walked off.

I shook my head, smiling to myself as I made my way across campus to the student medical center and, eventually, Gunnar. With every step I took, my unease grew, my memory of the moving shadows creeping back in. By the time I hit the lobby of the building, my anxiety had hit fever pitch. I barely said two words to the girl behind the desk before launching myself into Gunnar's office. Thank God she'd said it was okay to go in, though I wasn't sure it would have changed anything if she hadn't.

Gunnar looked up from his desk when I busted into the room.

"Eve? I didn't see you on the schedule today."

"Yeah, I had a conflict. It's gone now, and what's-her-name just squeezed me in. I called early this morning, but nobody was here. This is the only time she could fit me in."

His expression tightened, his brows scrunched with irritation. He grabbed a piece of paper from a notepad and scribbled something on it before getting up and handing it to me.

"Here. This is my cell number. I want you to use it if you need anything, okay?"

"Cool."

"And I mean *anything*, Eve," he said again, driving his point home.

"Yeah, I got it. Thanks."

"Now, do you want to have a seat and tell me what had you calling early this morning?"

No.

"Sure..." I made my way over to the sofa and dropped my bag beside it before sitting down. "You want me to just blurt it out or set the scene first?"

"Which would you prefer?"

Neither.

"So last night, after I got home from my date, I was closing the blinds in my room, and when I looked out my window, I swore I saw something moving in the trees below my apartment. I completely freaked out. I couldn't sleep. In the morning, I called to see you."

"What do you think you saw?" he asked, sitting down in the chair across from me.

"I have no fucking clue. Something—maybe someone?"

"Do you often feel like you see things?"

"Not often, no."

"Have you ever felt that way?"

He was tugging at the lock on the box of secrets I wanted to keep shut away. The short answer was yes. The long answer was something I really didn't want to get into with him.

When he saw my reluctance to answer, he switched gears.

Eve of Eternal Night

"You mentioned you had a date last night," he said, settling back into his chair. "How do you think it went?"

I leaned back against the sofa cushion to mimic his posture.

"It was fine."

"Just fine?"

"I mean... he was nice. Funny. Really funny, actually. We had dinner. He took me home. The end."

Gunnar stared at me, absorbing what I'd said and analyzing it, as was his job.

"Do you want to see him again?"

"I don't know. Maybe."

"How would you feel if he asked you out again?"

Normal.

"Good, I guess." I looked past him at a painting hanging on the wall behind his desk. The flow of the watercolor was mesmerizing, the pastels blending in such a way that I couldn't tell where one stopped and the other started.

"Eve?"

"Yeah," I said, snapping my attention back to him.

"You seem distracted today. Is there something else you'd prefer to focus on during our time? Something you haven't mentioned yet?"

Out of nowhere, an image of the shady rocker from the Sketchy Fox flashed in my mind, and my whole body went tight with fear and anticipation. I closed my eyes and imagined the feel of his body near mine. I bit my lip and forced myself to come back to the moment and not embarrass myself in front of Gunnar. As it was, he was looking at me strangely, a hint of concern in his eyes.

Or was it something else?

"Are you feeling well today, Eve?" he asked, shifting

forward in his seat to get a better look at me—or to get closer.

"Yeah, sorry. I'm just a bit tired. What were you saying?"

"I asked if there was something else you wanted to talk about today." *Want to? No. Not really.* "Or maybe there's a hypothetical you'd like to discuss. Something going on with someone else—someone other than you?"

Though I could see what he was doing—allowing me a chance to discuss my problem without actually owning it—I appreciated the gesture nonetheless. The truth was, I had no idea what to make of any feelings I had for Fenris or Stian or the rocker, for that matter. And some of those feelings were not necessarily healthy. I was out of my depth, my reactions to the three of them going against every policy I'd put in place over the years to keep myself safe. I was in desperate need of some sage advice from an objective party. Gunnar was the perfect sounding board. He always seemed to say the right thing, even when he pushed me. That was an art form as far as I was considered. I'd never met someone who could do it without overstepping.

And that never ended well.

"Let's say there's this girl—a friend of mine. She's potentially heading down a dangerous road with her life, and she knows it, but she can't seem to stop herself."

"Why is the road dangerous?"

"Because she's letting her guard down with people against her better judgment."

"Maybe that's okay—to let her guard down. To let someone in."

"Or maybe it's a train wreck waiting to happen."

He leaned closer still. "There's only one way to find out."

The hard set of his features contrasted with the softness of his gaze. For a moment, I found myself a bit lost in it.

Eve of Eternal Night

Drawn toward it. I shook my head, trying to break the trance I was in.

"What if she's drawn to three different guys—for completely different reasons—but she barely knows them?"

Gunnar sat up straighter, giving me more space.

"The only way to get to know someone better is to see them, learn more about them."

I laughed at that. "That might work for two of them, but the third? I don't think so. I'm not sure it'll work for any of them, really."

"Let's talk about why you think that is."

"Why? Because one is so eccentric that it's impossible to figure him out. The second is so eager that I can't help but question his motives at times. And the third one—" I cut myself off, trying to figure out how to describe the attraction to the rocker, other than the thrill of danger making my panties want to drop.

Silence drew out between us until Gunnar broke it.

"Where did she meet this third one?"

"At a bar."

"And she likes him?"

"She's... *intrigued* by him."

"In what way?"

He sat forward again, but this time there was no softness in his stare.

"There's just an attraction there—an unhealthy one. Purely physical."

"Has she acted on it?"

I shook my head emphatically. "No. He's trouble. She knows that much."

"But you think she doesn't care enough to stay away?" he asked. I nodded. "Okay. Let's work from the assumption that he isn't as dangerous as she thinks he is. How could she learn more in a safe way?"

I shrugged. "Go see him again at the bar?"

"Are you worried that your *friend* will get hurt?"

"... Maybe."

"In what way?"

"I don't know," I replied, fidgeting under the weight of his stare. The pretense of our conversation was eroding by the second. "Emotionally? Physically? Both? I don't know. I just feel like I should know better, and yet I don't seem to. I don't know why I want to pursue him, but I do."

"Maybe there is a reason why you're drawn to these particular individuals, Eve. Maybe you feel they balance something in you—something that you're missing?"

"What does that say about me, then, huh? That I'm totally fucked in the head? Because who in their right mind seeks out someone dark and disturbing—someone guaranteed to screw them up worse than they already are—and says 'yep. He's a keeper!'?"

Gunnar frowned at me, leaning forward to rest his forearms on his knees.

"Wanting something that seems destructive doesn't make you fucked in the head, Eve. It means you likely have unresolved feelings about something else, and those drive you to find comfort in a volatile situation. It's not rational, but it's hardly unheard of."

"Like I'm self-sabotaging?"

"Maybe. But I think it might be deeper than that. That's what we need to figure out."

"How do we go about that?" I asked, sounding a bit more desperate than I'd expected.

"Well this might sound unconventional, but you could—in a safe and controlled environment—meet with this individual and see if you can figure out what it is about him that you're attracted to. If we could isolate that, it might be helpful."

"Yeah... I don't think he's really a 'controlled environment' kind of guy. And I don't think he likes me at all. I think he enjoyed fucking with me. Or would like to fuck me, but that would likely be a one-hit wonder kind of situation."

"Do you think you're being fair to him in that assessment?"

"Yes. Most definitely, which makes my inability to get him out of my head even worse."

Gunnar's expression tightened a bit with what appeared to be frustration. Whom he was frustrated with, though, was beyond me—maybe himself for not having a better way to deal with my problem.

"Let me ask you this to see if we can weigh out your feelings for this person. Would you risk your budding relationship with the boy you went on the date with to continue down this unknown path with the dangerous guy? Or possibly the enigmatic one?"

That was an excellent question. One I didn't have an answer for.

"I don't know... they're all just so different. It's like they appeal to completely different sides of me." I paused for a second, trying to really put thought behind my words. "Do you think some of me is normal and the rest is... damaged beyond repair?"

"No, Eve. I don't think anyone is damaged beyond repair."

"You clearly haven't met my father," I muttered under my breath.

"Do you want to talk about him?"

"Hellllllll no!" I replied, practically jumping out of my

seat. "I'll talk about the sketchy dude all day long, but my dad? No way. Push me on that and I'll walk out that door and never come back."

"We don't have to talk about him if you're not ready to."

"Ready? It has nothing to do with ready. It has everything to do with not wanting to waste my time."

"I understand," he said, letting silence hang between us. I squirmed as I stood there, hating the growing quiet more and more with every passing second. Just about the time I wanted to jump out of my own skin, Gunnar spoke. His words shocked the hell out of me. "I know it's not my job to influence your choices, Eve. I'm a listening ear and a sounding board for your thought process. So you can take this as an off-the-record kind of statement if you want to, but your feelings about your father seem to influence every aspect of your life, and your desire to run from that truth is only going to cause you more hurt, not the opposite.

"Whether you choose the bad boy or the eager one or the eccentric one doesn't really matter. What matters is that you are in full control of your decision-making skills when you choose. If not, you're still letting your father rule your life."

I stared at him with wide eyes, uncertain as to whether I should be in awe or furious at what he'd just said. He'd way overstepped his role as my therapist, but I couldn't shake the feeling that he'd done so because he was worried I would do something dumb because of my daddy issues. Any choice could be driven by them, if I were being honest. Fenris represented normalcy—the kind I'd never had growing up. A stand-up guy who wanted to protect me. Bad boy, on the other hand, represented everything my father hated—and that fact brought me joy just thinking about it. And Stian? He was freedom from consequence, pure and simple.

"Time's up for today," Gunnar said, getting up out of his seat.

His announcement startled me from my thoughts. I checked my phone for the time, realizing it was five past the hour. I collected my belongings and made my way to the door with Gunnar right behind me. I paused before opening it, causing him to nearly bump into me. Instead of backing up, he hovered close to me. There was something comforting about having him at my back. Familiar, even.

"We never did figure out the shadow man thing," I said, looking over my shoulder at him. "Do you think it means something?"

"Yes," he said, reaching around me to open the door. "I do."

He said nothing else, so I made my way out, tossing a wave over my shoulder.

"What the fuck am I supposed to do with that?" I mumbled to myself as I exited the building. Gunnar had hardly been the fountain of wisdom I'd hoped for. Our conversation's digression into my love life, though welcome at the time, had done nothing to help me with answers. Maybe he thought that my relationships were a bigger concern, though I couldn't fathom why. Whom I dated seemed to pale in comparison to me hallucinating.

Maybe I needed another sounding board, one with a mind too linear to be distracted by anything but the facts. Given the time of morning, I knew where I could find just that, so I made my way to the chem building on a clear mission.

I needed to talk to Charlie.

12

"Hey Charlie," I said, poking my head into the lab. Charlie was always there, working on masters-level projects, though she was still an undergrad. The girl was too smart for her own good. I fondly remembered the day I asked her if she ever watched the Kardashians on TV, and she told me she didn't like sci-fi shows. It was like the sun had shone down upon us both, forging a bond.

She looked away from whatever she was working on under the hood and gave a quick wave before returning her attention to the chemicals she was working with. Probably for the best. Causing an explosion wasn't really my goal. I'd tracked her down for another reason.

I waited patiently until she was done, stacking some dried test tubes in their holder. She walked over to me about five minutes later, pulling her goggles off her face. The red rings they left behind always made me giggle.

"Is there something I can help you with, Eve?" she asked, pushing her unruly hair off her face.

"Do you have a minute?"

"Oh yes. Fifteen minutes to be exact." I smiled at her precise answer. Chemistry dictated her schedule—literally. "Does this have to do with your TA position?"

"No, not that. It's about—" I cut myself off, trying to decide how best to present my concern in a methodical and logical way. That was the language she spoke. Anything abstract and she just shut down, unable to think beyond black and white. "Charlie... do you think it's possible to think you've seen something but not have *actually* seen it?"

"The neuroscience community has long stated that the mind doesn't actually know the difference between what's real—an actual concrete experience—and one that has been vividly imagined. So I think it's very possible that someone can recall an event or moment in time as though it happened when it in fact didn't."

That answer was not comforting.

"You mean I could have had a dream and woken up and thought it was real?"

"It's more complicated than that, but in theory, yes. You could have." She looked at me for a moment, her sharp brown eyes staring me down. "Am I to assume that we aren't speaking hypothetically? That you're asking about this because of something that happened to you?"

I nodded. "I need you to promise me that you won't say a word." She pulled away from me, the offense she'd taken at my words clear in her expression.

"I would never do that to you—unless you'd done something illegal. Then I would be obligated to report you."

"Good news there because I didn't."

"Then tell me what you think you saw."

I took a deep breath, looking over my shoulder to the door as I took a step closer to her. Her body tensed with my proximity so I halted, not pressing any nearer.

"A body..."

"A body? Like someone's naked body?"

"No," I said, shaking my head. I knew I should have been more specific. "Like a dead one."

Her eyes went a bit wide when those words registered.

"Were you in the anatomy lab at the med school?"

"I would have expected to see one there, Charlie. It was between two of the frat houses on Greek Row the other night. During some big party."

"Perhaps the individual had just passed out."

"I don't think so. I could see blood, Charlie. Lots of it. And... and I think I saw the people who killed him. They were still standing around him when I saw them—like they'd just murdered him."

"Were you intoxicated?"

"It was a party. Of course I was, but I wasn't hammered. My blood alcohol level has nothing to do with this."

"Studies have shown that even a point zero—"

"Charlie!" I shouted, cutting off her scientific ramblings. "I wasn't even a little drunk. I know what I saw. I'd swear to it in a court of law."

She assessed me for a moment, then nodded as if she were satisfied.

"Did you inform the authorities?"

"Yes! Right after I locked myself in my apartment. When I woke up the next day, I didn't see anything about a murder on the news. Nothing in my email about a crime committed on campus."

"Maybe they moved the body," she said matter of factly. I had to give her points for that one. I hadn't even considered that option; it would explain a lot. All except for the total lack of crime scene at the scene of the crime.

Eve of Eternal Night

"How? Someone would have seen them the second they emerged from between those two buildings."

"Someone inebriated."

"That's one hell of a risk, don't you think? Drunk co-eds or otherwise?"

She looked thoughtful for a moment before checking her watch. "Maybe they waited until the party had ended."

"Charlie, those parties don't ever really end. They might die down a bit, but people would have been going strong until the sun came up."

"Perhaps that wouldn't have been a logical move, then," she seemed to say to herself. She walked over to the hood where her experiment was reacting, gave it a cursory glance, then made her way back to me. "So your working theory is what? That either what you saw didn't actually happen, or it did happen and there's some sort of conspiracy to cover it up?"

Damn... she'd used the 'c' word. Charlie was way too literal in thought to believe in such things. If she thought that was my suggestion, our conversation would be over, never to be broached again.

"Of course I don't think it's a conspiracy. I just don't know how to reconcile what I'm sure I saw with the lack of an actual crime."

"Did you take a picture of the criminals?"

"Um, no, I didn't. I was too busy trying not to freak the fuck out and running away."

"That would have been really helpful to prove that you didn't just imagine it somehow."

"Trust me, I'm well aware of how inconvenient my desire to not be murdered is now."

She frowned at me for a moment, likely trying to process my sarcasm. "Your desire to live is hardly inconvenient, Eve.

It's an evolutionary necessity. Without it, our species would cease to exist."

I groaned audibly. "I know that, Charlie. What I'm saying is that my desire to live is now biting me in the ass because I don't have proof of what I saw that night."

"Oh, yes. That makes more sense now."

"So... what do I do?"

"Nothing," she replied without skipping a beat.

"Nothing?"

"Yes. Why?"

"Because 'nothing' doesn't really help me process this."

"Then don't try to process it at all."

"You think I should just try to forget it?"

"I think you are expending an exorbitant amount of energy and time on a puzzle that, by nature of its missing pieces, can never be solved."

The nerd had a point.

"How do you forget something like that, though? I mean, seriously?"

"Find something else to focus on. Or someone."

"A distraction?"

"Yes. At least one, if not more."

Just as I opened my mouth to reply, the alarm on her watch started chirping, telling us both that our conversation was over. Charlie strode over to the hood and smiled at what she saw. At that moment, I knew I'd lost her to her experiment.

"Thanks Charlie," I said over my shoulder as I walked to the door. As expected, I didn't hear anything in return. Charlie was not a multitasker in the 'can't walk and chew gum' sort of way.

I stepped out into the empty hall and put my messenger bag over my shoulder. In some way, my chat with Charlie had made me feel a bit better. She hadn't said I was crazy, so that was a plus, but she had pointed out some plausible alternatives about that night that I wasn't in the mood to consider. Her idea to try and forget was an inviting one, to say the least. But I knew the second I closed my eyes, the image of those five men hovering over the body would likely come to me, and I would know no peace. If I had any chance of relying on distractions to help myself forget, I was going to need a whole shitload of them. Copious amounts. Boatloads, even.

Then I pushed open the main entrance to the building that faced out into the common area and saw one walking toward me.

13

"Eve!" Fenris called, jogging the few yards separating us to join me.

"Hey," I replied, smiling back at him. His boyish charm was undeniable.

"So, I had fun last night."

"You had fun torturing me with laughter."

He grinned.

"I really did. I'd like to do it again sometime."

"Was that your attempt at asking me on a second date?"

"Yep."

I shook my head as I laughed.

"Maybe. But right now I have papers to grade and classes to go to."

"What are you doing tonight?"

"No clue. I'm not really a planner."

"Well I'm going to call you later and hit you with a bullet-point outline highlighting all the reasons you should hang out with me tonight."

I laughed again. "Why do I get the feeling you're not joking about that?"

He stepped closer to me, tucking a stray lock of hair behind my ear as it whipped in the wind.

"Because I take some things very seriously." His blue eyes lingered on mine until I caved and looked away. How someone so goofy could be so intense was bizarre. "I'll call you later."

He hovered near me, his body close, before walking away. I felt a pang of something as he did—something uncomfortable. Something I hadn't noticed when he was standing in front of me. I took a few deep breaths, wondering if I just needed to calm my system, but the feeling remained.

※

By the time I was finished with classes and grading, it was dinnertime. I grabbed something from the cafeteria, not sure I had anything at home to make, and walked back to my apartment. I checked my messages on the way and found one from Fenris. He really had put together a bullet-point outline.

I thought about calling him back, about taking him up on his offer to take me out, but the truth was, I had something else in mind. Despite Charlie's distraction suggestion, I needed to tuck myself away at the bar and drown my wandering thoughts in tequila long enough for my mind to still. Sleep was becoming evasive, making it harder and harder to think clearly. Even the classes I'd prided myself on acing that semester were starting to fall by the wayside. All because of the memory I couldn't erase.

The memory of five killers and a missing dead body.

That part of town was busy for a Tuesday, forcing me to park three blocks over from the Sketchy Fox. It wasn't as if I hadn't made that journey before. But with the rise in crime and my mind in a dark place, it felt much more dubious than normal.

I locked my car and slung my purse over my shoulder to hang across my body. Tucking my keys into my black leather bag, I walked down the sidewalk, sticking to the curbside edge. The buildings seemed to loom above me in a nefarious way, as though their doors would fly open at any moment and suck me in to some terrible, unspeakable fate; one that wouldn't make the news, just like the murder I'd seen. I shivered at the thought and drew my jacket closed. Even then, the cold seemed to permeate me in a way I couldn't escape.

Two blocks up, I turned down the side street where the bar was located. The streetlights hung overhead, dark and dormant. It was like the city hadn't bothered to turn them on. Like that part of town wasn't worthy of illumination. My steps quickened to match the beat of my heart as I neared the bar. My unease was starting to swallow me whole. I knew if I could just get there and start drinking, all would be right with the world.

But I didn't just get there—so it wasn't.

A few buildings before I reached the Sketchy Fox, I heard a strangled cry from a darkened alcove to my right. Like an idiot, I stopped to see what was there. Through the shadows, I could make out a form hovering over a body. Déjà vu shot through me. But instead of letting my instincts kick in, I stood fast and reached into my bag for my phone. Come hell or high water, I was getting evidence this time.

"Hey!" I shouted, holding up my phone. "Say cheese, motherfucker."

I snapped a picture with the flash. The screen lit up with a gruesome sight, one my mind struggled yet again to reconcile. But this time, it couldn't deny what it saw. It had to own that a corpse lay at a man's feet, covered in blood. And the murderer, his face sharp and rugged and beautiful, stared back at me with black, lifeless eyes.

My phone crashed to the ground.

I was in a dead sprint for the bar before I thought that maybe I should have tried to collect my evidence first. But the man had lunged out of the darkness at me and I'd freaked, which was understandable given the situation. My feet slapped hard against the concrete and my arms pumped wildly at my sides. I was so close—only fifteen yards or so until I could find sanctuary amid the misfits of the city. But I could feel the cold brush of something on the back of my neck, and I wondered if it was already too late. If I was already slated to die.

I looked back over my shoulder, expecting to see my killer smiling back at me, but there was no one there. When I turned to face forward again, I slammed into someone standing in front of the bar who hadn't been there two seconds before. I stumbled backward, prepared to fall on my ass, but strong hands caught me by my leather jacket and hauled me upright.

Instinctively, I swatted at his hold, my adrenaline clouding my judgment. Everything in that moment was a threat. Even the person trying to help me.

"Latte girl?" he said, drawing my attention to his face. His brow was creased with worry and confusion. "What are you doing here?"

"Did you see him?" I gasped, still trying to catch my breath. "Did you see the guy chasing me?"

"I just came outside for a smoke," he said, holding up his cigarettes. "Next thing I knew, you crashed into me like a freight train."

"Come with me," I said, grabbing him by the hand. I dragged him back down the sidewalk toward the alcove where I'd seen the body. He followed behind me without question, which might have seemed odd if it were anyone else. But Stian was odd to say the least, so he said nothing at all. When we reached the building, I stepped carefully toward where the victim's body had been. But even in the scant light of the moon, I could see that it was gone. Nothing but a concrete step was there.

"I don't understand," I whispered to myself.

"I'm always up for an adventure, but I don't really see the appeal of this one," he said, amusement in his tone.

"I saw a man kill someone in here. I was running for my life when I plowed into you," I shouted, wheeling around to face him. "I don't find that funny, do you?"

His expression sobered. He put a cigarette to his lips and lit up, taking a long drag before pulling it away. Seconds later, he exhaled a cloud of smoke that seemed to wind through the air like a dancer before disappearing entirely. He walked toward me, appraising me as he did.

"You saw someone killed? In here?"

"I swear I did. I know it sounds crazy, but—"

"Not in this neighborhood, it doesn't."

"I know I saw it." Realization dawned on me hard. I had taken a picture of the crime. I had proof this time. "My phone!" I exclaimed, darting past Stian to where I'd dropped it. I searched everywhere, wondering if the murderer or I had kicked it somewhere when we'd taken off. But all I managed to find was a single Swarovski crystal that had broken off the case. Feeling dejected, I crumpled down onto the curb and buried my head in my hands. "It's gone. I dropped it and now it's gone." Then I shot back up, panic surging through me. "What if he took it? What if he can crack my security code? He could find me... he knows I saw him!"

"Shh," Stian said, gently grabbing my arm to stop my flailing. "Even if he did take your phone, he's not going to get through your code, okay?"

His serious stare seemed to calm my agitation.

He loomed before me for a moment before pulling me down to sit beside him on the curb. He said nothing, just continued to smoke. After a while, he offered me a drag, and I gladly took it. The burning in my throat felt good—made me feel alive.

"You're sure you got a picture of the crime?" he asked, his voice calm and normal, as if he weren't asking about evidence of a murder.

"I did. I saw the murderer in the flash."

A pause.

"What did he look like?"

"Beautiful... terrifying..."

"Can you describe him beyond that?"

"Yeah, but why? To whom?"

He pulled out a pad of paper from his back pocket.

"Got a pen in that massive bag of yours?" he asked with a wry smile. Something about it seemed to calm me, if only a little. I reached in and rummaged around until I found one and handed it over to him.

For the next ten minutes or so, Stian asked me pointed questions about the killer's features. Because that flash photo seemed to still be seared into my brain, I was able to give him what I thought was an adequate description. When he was done scribbling on the pad of paper, he ripped the page free and gave it to me. I gasped at the sight. The image looking back at me was a perfect rendering of the killer.

"That's him," I said under my breath. "Oh my God, that's

him!" I jumped up and looked down at Stian, who sat there quietly. "We have to take this to the police! We have to get it on the news!"

"There is nothing we can do. Other than this picture of someone you may or may not have seen, we have no proof. The cops will take your statement and then do nothing. I know how this works."

"But... but I can't just sit on this. I know what I saw!"

"And you can't prove it. Proof is what matters. Not truth." He tucked the notepad away in his pocket, then stood up to face me. Even standing on the road below the curb, he was still taller than me. His grey eyes peered into mine in the darkness, trying to read something in them that I wasn't sure he could see. "Come have a drink with me," he said, still staring into what little soul I still had left. "Or maybe three."

I choked on a laugh. "I think tonight is a five-drink minimum for sure."

"Come on," he said, taking my hand in his. The warmth of it soothed me, releasing the vise strangling my heart. Breathing felt easier with every inhalation, and my pulse slowed to a non-coronary event level. His thumb stroked my wrist, practically coaxing my blood to slow. "What's your poison?"

"Tequila. Top-shelf shit."

He looked down the street at the bar, then back to me. "I'm not sure this place has a top shelf, but we can hope."

"It does. I'm a regular at the Sketchy Fox."

His sly smile reminded me of one. "Well, well, latte girl, you really are full of surprises."

I smiled back. "*Eve*. My name is Eve."

"Eve..." he repeated, his voice wistful as he spoke. "I like that."

He stepped up onto the curb and led me toward the bar. With every step I took away from the crime scene, it started to fade from my mind, until I could just barely grasp the memory if I tried really hard.

"Why are you here?" I asked him, letting my lazy gaze drift up to his face.

He looked down at me and laughed, shaking his head. "Simple," he said, pulling the door open. "I'm here for the band."

We found spots at the bar and he quickly excused himself, heading down the hall toward the bathrooms, cell phone in hand. Cheryl spotted me and made her way over, bottle of tequila at the ready.

"Here a bit early tonight, aren't ya?" Cheryl plopped a tumbler down in front of me and poured my drink.

"It's been a rough week. I needed to take the edge off."

She looked at me with the shrewdness of a woman who'd lived a tough life and seen things I hoped to never see.

"Taking the edge off wouldn't involve a certain leather-clad lead singer, would it?" Her sharp eyes narrowed at me. "One who loves pretty girls sitting alone at the bar?"

"I'm not alone," I said, then looked at the spot Stian had vacated moments earlier. I peered down the hall but didn't see him.

"You look pretty damn alone to me," she replied. "And I know what lonely girls do around guys like him."

I scoffed and took a swig of my tequila. "That guy's a piece of work."

"A damn fine one to look at," she said with a wry smile. "But you should believe me when I tell you, you ain't woman enough to handle someone like Godric, no matter how much you think you are. He'd eat you up and spit you out so fast your head would spin."

"I can handle myself," I told her, taking another drink.

"Oh I'm sure you can, but he's not one you want to underestimate. You're the kind of girl who grew up around white-collar crime. Ain't nothin' white collar about him."

"I don't plan on messing with him, Cheryl, so I think I'll be good."

She stared at me while she dried the already dry glass in her hand.

"Just watch yourself, kid. I don't want to see you get hurt —and not just your feelings, if you know what I mean." She turned to place the glass on the bar behind her before looking over her shoulder at me. "You're a good one, Eve. Don't let him ruin that."

She walked away to tend to someone at the far end of the bar, but her sentiments still hung in the air. If Cheryl said the surly rocker was bad news, then he was, plain and simple. But my mind couldn't help but wonder just how bad he was, or how much Cheryl really knew about him—the specifics of why he was such a danger to a girl like me. Had I been a virgin or naïve, I could see her point about certain things he might pose a threat to, but I was neither.

And her warnings about him only piqued my interest further.

As if on cue, I looked up to see the man in question striding down the narrow hallway Stian had disappeared down. He was headed for the bar, and more pointedly, me. I held my ground against his approach, acting indifferent when I felt anything but. Something about being around him made me feel alive, the heady combination of fear and lust and adrenaline coursing through me like a freight train. My chest tightened when his eyes met mine, and I knew in that instant that Cheryl's words no longer carried any weight.

I was going to play with fire even knowing I'd get burned.

"You again," he said, leaning against the bar in Stian's spot. "Twice isn't a coincidence, you know."

"This has been my Friday night spot for the past year, and if memory serves, I never saw you here before last week. If this isn't a coincidence, then that's on you."

Happy with my retort, I turned away from him and leaned my elbows on the bar. I picked up my glass and held it in front of me for a beat, swirling the tequila around a few times before I took a sip. I let it sit in my mouth for a moment before swallowing slowly, letting the burn creep down my throat.

"But it's Tuesday," he replied, the heavy weight of his stare bearing down on me. "So that raises the question: why are you here off your normal schedule?"

When I hazarded a glance to my side, I found him smiling at me, eyes assessing me in a non-sexual way. That got my attention, and I turned to face him, hardening my gaze to match his. If we were playing a game, I had no intention of letting him win so easily.

"You calling me a stalker?" I asked, managing not to flinch when his features tightened.

"Hardly. I'm calling it like I see it; you're seeking me out. But I wonder... why would a girl like you choose a place like this? Was it because your daddy didn't love you, or because you think you're tough when really you're just a scared little girl playing at being hard?"

"And what did you decide?" I asked, feigning interest.

"I think both might apply."

"Let me guess, you have the perfect way of finding out.

Something about you and me and a locked bathroom in the back of the bar. If so, you're going to be disappointed when my date returns."

He laughed at my response, a raspy, rugged sound that seemed to echo over the din of the bar. It wrapped around me like a noose and tightened until I could barely breathe. At first, I thought there was something wrong with me. Then I realized that his hand was on my knee, and my reaction made so much more sense. I watched motionless as it slid up my thigh, higher and higher, until it bordered on public indecency—even in an establishment as dubious as the Sketchy Fox.

"You were saying," he said, prompting me to continue when he could clearly see I was flustered. He'd called my bluff with a single pass of his hand. Maybe Cheryl had been right. Maybe I was beyond out of my league toying with this one.

I was a kitten. He was a lion.

"Stop touching me," I said, my words barely audible over the music in the bar. I hoped it disguised just how breathy and wanton I sounded.

His hand stayed firmly planted on my thigh.

"I hate to tell you this, but you don't look—or sound—like that's what you really want," he said, leaning closer to me. "I know what you like…"

A vision of him leaning over me, his face shrouded in shadow, laughing, flashed through my mind. Panic shot through me and my heart pounded against my ribs, my fight-or-flight response in overdrive for the second time that evening. But there was a part of me—something buried deep inside—that wondered if there wasn't a third 'f' response that might have been applicable in that moment, if fight, flight, or fuck wasn't a thing. Because even though I was scared as hell, I really didn't want him to stop.

I swallowed hard against my tightening throat, moving my leg out from under his grip. I turned back to the bar to find Cheryl there, her eyes glued to me. She was looking for something—a sign that I needed her help, most likely. I shook my head at her, then slammed my drink. With a turn of the stool and a hop down, I walked toward the exit. I didn't bother to look back at the wild ride watching me leave. He'd made his point, and I had way too much pride to let him see how much his win bothered me.

I was sure he was having a good laugh at my expense regardless.

The cool night air helped calm me a bit as I walked to my car. Stupid, I thought, letting my hormones dictate my decisions. Those assholes had left me in a pickle more times than I could count. And that was before my life had gone to shit. Now they had me walking up the street I'd fled down to escape a murder I was sure I'd witnessed but was no longer so certain about. Seeing that alcove devoid of blood or a corpse made my head spin, my heart race, and my pace quicken.

I needed to get home.

As I walked, I wondered if I'd ever learn to leave well enough alone. I already knew the answer to that—probably not—but I pondered it anyway. When it came to guys like him, all bets were off. The ginger genes in me ran too deep to not be ruled by my emotions. Backing down was not in my nature.

Poking a bear with a short stick was.

Once I reached my car, I realized I'd walked out on Stian. Just up and bolted without a word. For a second, I contemplated going back to the bar, but I shot that down. I knew I couldn't bear to see the look on the bad boy's face if I returned. It would only egg him on—make him think that I wanted him like he assumed I did. And it was that assumption that was making my blood boil.

Or maybe it was the fact that it was correct.

I drove off, hoping I'd see Stian the next day on campus. I owed him an apology of epic proportions, not only for bailing on him, but also for my behavior in the street. I still didn't have an explanation for that, and I was really starting to wonder if my mind had conjured up the whole thing. I hadn't imagined my missing phone, though. That was real enough. But in that neighborhood, a cell phone on the sidewalk would have been scooped up in a heartbeat. No surprise there.

The tequila started to kick in just as I arrived home, and I hoped it would bring sleep with it. But when I laid my head down, all I could see were flashes of what I thought I'd seen that night in the storefront alcove. Dark black eyes boring through me—calling to me. I woke up several times that night to check the locks on my door and windows. I couldn't shake the feeling that I was being stalked somehow. Hunted. Watched.

After the fifth time, I grabbed a bottle of tequila from the kitchen and brought it back to bed with me, proceeding to drink until the dark eyes were eclipsed by a feeling of warmth and the need to pass out.

14

I woke up feeling like shit. Actually, 'woke up' implied that I'd slept, which I wasn't sure I had. Passed out, yes, but not slept. I felt exhausted, with a lingering hangover that promised to get worse before it got better. Just as I was about to vow to never drink again, I remembered why I'd started pounding shots of tequila in the first place.

I'd witnessed another murder.

I ran to the living room in search of my cell phone, clutching my forehead to try and quell the stabbing pain I felt. I'd taken a picture of it this time—that much I knew. But the second I opened my purse to search for it, the memory of dropping it as I fled the scene slapped me. It was long gone.

"Dammit," I said, throwing my purse at the door. That picture would have blown any doubts I had about what I'd seen that night out of the water. The night in Greek Row too, for that matter. I couldn't imagine physical evidence into existence. Even Charlie couldn't argue that.

But she could argue that I imagined taking the picture in the first place...

Then I looked over at the door, where the contents of my purse lay strewn about the floor. A folded piece of white paper nearly shouted at me to pick it up. I walked over and plucked it up, unfolding it as I did. My heart skipped a beat when I looked down at the face of the murderer I'd seen last night.

Panic crept in around me. I dropped the sketch to the floor like it had burned me, and I tugged at the collar of my T-shirt, trying to breathe. I suddenly needed to get out of my apartment—far away from that sketch. I needed to be in a large space with lots of people. Lots of potential witnesses.

I ran to my room, threw on a hoodie over my shirt, and pulled on some jeans. A pair of sneakers later, I was ready to go. It was later in the morning than I'd realized (hangovers will do that), so I had class in twenty minutes.

As I made my way to campus, I realized that losing my phone posed more of an issue than not having the evidence I needed, or the potential for the murderer to track me. It also meant that I didn't have a phone. I had a break after teaching, which would give me enough time to run to the store to get a new one. With that plan in mind, I made my way to the chemistry building, reeking of booze and cigarettes.

I threw my things down on the desk and started to unpack until something in the back of the room caught my eye. A familiar face was smiling at me when I looked up at him. *Fenris...* My day was about to get a whole lot more interesting.

He started toward me, and I looked down to dig through my backpack, looking for my teaching textbook.

"Hey," he said, sidling up next to me.

"You're not in this class," I said, not looking up at him.

"I am now. I had my schedule changed."

"Fenris... you do know we have stalking laws in this state, right?"

"Yep. I'm well versed in them." I craned my head to stare at him. The mischievous grin on his face told me he'd gotten me yet again. "You shouldn't flatter yourself so much, Eve. I just switched because the other TA is the worst."

Charlie.

"Yeah, I could see how you two wouldn't be a good match."

"So I had this period free and got switched over."

"Great. Take a seat, then." I stared at him, hoping his satisfaction with his schedule change would eventually fall from his expression, but it did no such thing. He just stared back, the twinkle in his eyes making me more flustered by the second. Just about the time I thought I'd snap, he made his way back to his seat.

I took a deep breath and let it out with a harsh blow.

My day was off to a banner start.

※

THAT FELT like the longest hour of my life. For some reason, everyone and their cousin had questions, both during and after class. The more my head throbbed and begged for aspirin, the more they wanted to know about Fischer projections and carbon bonds and I don't even know what else because I just stopped listening. I caught Fenris leaning against the wall by the door, laughing to himself—laughing at my personal hell. For a minute, I seriously considered walking over and kneeing him in the balls.

Once the mob of eager beavers filed out, leaving him and me alone, he sauntered over.

"Rough night, huh?"

I stiffened at his words. "You have no idea."

He gently placed his hand on my forearm and drew my focus away from the papers on my desk. "Do you want to talk about it?"

I shook my head. "Not really. I've got to go."

"Anywhere in particular?"

"Somewhere to get a new cell phone—I lost mine last night."

"Want me to take you? I have some time before I need to be back here."

I opened my mouth to argue that I didn't need any company, then snapped it shut. I thought about how much fun I'd had with Fenris the other night. How hard he'd made me laugh. How normal I felt around him. And if there was anything I needed in that moment (other than a cell phone), it was normalcy.

And a sense of security, as thoughts of the previous night and the dark-eyed murderer pressed against my mind.

Fenris saw my hesitation and turned up the wattage on his smile.

"Sure. That'd be great. I left my car at home this morning, so it would save me the trek back there to get it. Thanks."

"No problem," he replied, hitching his bag up on his shoulder. "Shall we?"

I shook my head and laughed at him as I zipped mine shut. "Don't make me regret this, Fenris."

"As if that were even possible."

※

If I was being honest with myself, I didn't regret letting him take me. Getting a phone turned into lunch, then a matinee when I should have been in class. It was so comfortable being around him, like slipping into a well-worn leather jacket you'd had for years. You felt more complete with it on. Being around him just felt right.

He drove me home around dinnertime, after I turned down his offer to share that meal as well. I lingered in the SUV for a few seconds longer than I needed to, and when I turned to say goodbye to him, I was met with a weighted gaze. There were so many emotions in his eyes: hope, anticipation, desire. They were tinged with a bit of fear as well.

"Thanks for everything," I said, turning away from him quickly as I opened the door. "I'll see you later."

He reached across the car and caught my arm before I could get all the way out of the vehicle. His touch was gentle, and when I turned to face him, I found his expression was as well.

"Are you sure you're okay about whatever happened last night?"

I forced a smile at him. "I think I will be."

I stepped back and closed the door, then jogged across the street to my building. I unlocked it to the thrum of his engine as he waited for me to enter. I waved over my shoulder as I opened the door and stepped inside. Once I was in my apartment, I locked the door and flopped down on the couch, still exhausted. My hangover was gone, which was a mixed blessing. My head felt better, but it was also working more clearly—or what I thought was more clearly. Images of blood and darkness and empty eyes haunted my thoughts. I would have given anything to drown them out again.

I found the sketch Stian had done for me still laying on the floor, and I snatched it up. Seconds later, it was tucked safely away in a drawer, those eyes hidden from view. Unfortunately for me, they were already seared into my mind.

I turned on the TV to try and replace the images in my mind and landed on some cheesy romance movie. A mood-lifter, or so I hoped. It wasn't long before my eyelids grew heavy and sleep pulled me under. And tired though I was, I really wished it hadn't.

15

I dreamt of darkness. Of a great nothing. A vast wasteland.

I saw faceless bodies embroiled in a war that I was quick to join.

So much blood. So much death.

When it was over, I surveyed the scene with a sickening sense of satisfaction. Pride in the part I'd played. The carnage I'd created.

A flash of white light nearly blinded me. Even through closed eyelids, it was painful to behold. A voice accompanied it, loud and booming and foreboding, speaking in a language my subconscious mind seemed to understand but my brain couldn't process. It seemed to come from everywhere and nowhere alike.

I couldn't shake the familiarity of his tone. Even in sleep, it niggled at the back of my mind. A silhouette approached, blocking out some of the light that blinded me. I blinked hard, trying to make out his features, but they never came into focus. A wicked sword hung in his hand, and the closer he got to me, the higher he raised it.

"Next time, it will be you."

The sword came crashing down toward me. I closed my eyes and waited for my fate.

❧

I SHOT up on the couch, breathing hard, my heart beating wildly as I clutched my chest. It was dark outside, and I fumbled for my phone on the coffee table. 10:22 p.m. Apparently I'd been more exhausted than I thought.

I took a deep breath and tried to shake off the nightmare I'd had, tried to chalk it up to my damaged psyche. But there were too many of those events for a casual blow-off. Something was going on; something ominous that I couldn't ignore, even if I tried. Things hadn't gotten as bad as they had last time—when I turned eighteen—but they were toeing the line, and that made me nervous.

In the bathroom, I splashed water on my face and tried to clear my mind. I would not go down that road again. Not if I could help it. No, I was going to pull my shit together and get to the bottom of whatever was going on around me, and in my city, for that matter. Because it wasn't my imagination. It just wasn't.

I couldn't afford for it to be.

I'd stayed away from any kind of prescription drug since those days, knowing that it was that or spend the rest of my years in some sort of drug-induced numb zone where things weren't really any better—I just cared a lot less. Don't get me wrong; I *liked* that place. It was the path of least resistance for sure. But there was a part of me somewhere deep inside that had begged to be rid of the poison the doctors and my father had all too happily fed me. That had warned that they would be the death of me if I didn't stop. So one day—

Eve of Eternal Night

three months after my first episode—I woke up and threw them all out. The withdrawals were a special kind of hell that I wouldn't wish on anyone, but I managed to get through them. My father never even noticed.

My mind snapped back from its trip down memory lane and focused on the reflection before me in the medicine cabinet. My skin was sallow. The circles under my eyes were deep and black. I ran my fingertips along them as though I could force the bruised color away with one swipe.

"I need water," I said to myself, heading for the kitchen. "That'll help."

I pulled a bottle out of the fridge and started chugging. With the lights off, I stared out the window over the sink at the yard below, thinking about the shadow I'd seen there when I'd come back from my date with Fenris. Ice crept up my spine as the memory grew more vivid, but I stood my ground and continued to stare out into the darkness. I had to face the uncertainty of what I'd actually seen that night. I had to either accept or reject it and proceed from there. Same with the murders.

Though my bravado was strong, it started to wane when my weary eyes began to play tricks on me. Was that a branch or an arm that just moved? Someone running or a shadow stretching with the light of a passing car? Before I knew it, I was curled up on the couch again, clutching my phone. Panic started to course through me, and I shut my eyes, hoping I could tamp it back down—keep it from erupting. In that moment, all I wanted to feel was safe. The one thing I'd never felt when everything was too much and the world was crumbling down around me. I closed my eyes and tried to think of thoughts that made me feel happy and safe, but none came to mind—only the image of a person.

Fenris...

Around him, I felt secure. Safe. Protected.

Before I could overthink it, I called him.

"Hey you," he said. The warmth in his voice wrapped around me, easing the tension in my shoulders a bit. "What's up? Everything okay?"

"Yep," I replied a little too hastily. "Totally fine. I was just... having trouble sleeping, so I thought I'd see what you were up to. You know... try out my new phone."

He laughed, but it sounded forced. Like he saw right through me.

"And how do you like it?"

"I mean, I can hear you, so that's a plus."

Silence.

"Eve, are you sure you're okay?"

No. But telling him that I thought shadowy people were stalking me and murderers were lurking around every corner and, oh yeah, I might be having another break with reality seemed like a conversation killer, so I kept all that to myself and tried to think of something else that would satisfy his curiosity without sending him running.

"If I'm being honest, no. Not really."

"What's wrong?" The note of tension in his voice was clear.

And wasn't that the million-dollar question?

"Things are just really tense around here at the moment. I've had a couple of... *run-ins* that have left me a bit shaken."

"Run-ins with what?" he asked, his tone unchanged.

"It's complicated and not something I really want to go into." *Because I don't want to sound like I'm totally losing it.* "I'm just on edge, and being alone seems to make it worse."

More silence.

"Do you want me to come over?"

Yes.

"No, that's okay. I just thought maybe talking to you would distract me."

"Eve, it's no problem, really. I can come over."

"You just got rid of me!" I said, trying to make light of the situation.

"I didn't want to get rid of you, if you recall. I'd be happy to come over if it would make you feel better. And if you're worried about being alone in your apartment with me, don't be. I'll be on my best behavior. Promise."

"I feel like only people with ill intentions make promises like that."

"Then I take it back. I don't promise to behave at all. In fact, I'll be wildly inappropriate the whole time, and you'll wish I'd never come."

"Now that sounded a wee bit too honest for your own good," I said, covering my mouth to stifle the giggle that followed.

"So I'm damned if I do and damned if I don't, huh?"

"Maybe."

"Well then... maybe I should just go," he replied. Although he tried, he couldn't quite sell the hurt in his voice. I knew he was full of shit.

Looked like I'd beaten him for once. "Okay. Later—"

"Eve! Don't hang up."

"Yessss...?"

"I'm coming over. I'll be there in ten."

"But—"

He hung up on me.

Ten minutes later, on the nose, I heard him yelling at me from outside the building. I stuck my head out my living room window and shushed him.

"Will you stop shouting?"

"Will you let me in?"

I smiled wickedly. "You'll behave?"

He put his hand over his heart and made some archaic pledge to me—something about honor and virtue and not trying to separate me from my pants. He delivered it all with a straight face. I had to let him up after that performance. It seemed cruel not to.

"Fine! I'll buzz you in."

I hit the button long enough for him to open the door and waited for him to show up. I opened my apartment door to him smiling like he'd just won some battle I hadn't known we were having. He held a board game in his hands; one of those military strategy kinds that I hated.

"I think I should have left you outside," I said, standing in the entrance.

"Aw, c'mon. You're a nerd. I'm a nerd. I thought we could do nerdy things together."

"I am not a nerd!" I protested, letting him in.

"Right... that's why you're a chemistry TA. Got it. *Totally* not nerdy."

"Okay smartass. What makes you so nerdilicious?"

He shifted his gaze to me through hooded eyelids. "I'm smart. Really smart. And I'm going to kick your ass at this game."

There was a husky tone to his voice that made my chest tighten.

"We'll see about that."

※

"For the record," he said, clearing the board after my complete and utter annihilation, "you are the worst nerd ever. Were you even trying?"

"I was!" I shouted, throwing a plastic game piece at his head. It bounced off his forehead and fell into the box.

"It's like you have no idea how to fight a war," he muttered under his breath.

"Um, yeah. Because I *don't*. I'm a chemistry nerd, remember?"

He groaned in response as he cleaned up the game. Once he finished, he turned his baby blues to me.

"So... what now?"

I looked at my phone. It was half past midnight already. "Bedtime."

He quirked a brow at me. "And you told me to be on my best behavior. I'll have you know, Eve, I'm not that easy to get into bed."

I felt my cheeks flush and hated them for it. "I meant bedtime for *me*. Home for *you*."

"Ah, that makes more sense," he replied with a wink. He collected his game and made his way to the door. When he turned to say goodbye, he wore the serious expression I'd seen a few times before. It was then that I realized just how easy he was to read. He seemed incapable of hiding his emotions. We were complete opposites in that regard, but I found it refreshing. "Eve," he said, his hand resting on the doorknob, "if you feel better with me here, I could sleep on the couch—if that would give you peace of mind."

"You have class tomorrow at eight, I believe, and a test coming up soon that you should probably study for. Somehow I think if you stick around here, you'll talk me into a rematch, and neither one of us will get any sleep."

"Maybe," he replied with a shy smile.

He let go of the door and stepped toward me. Our bodies were close—too close—and I could feel warmth radiating off him. It was hard to stop myself from leaning into it.

"Fenris," I said softly.

"Eve." His tone perfectly matched my own.

"I can't do this."

"Do what?" he asked, leaning in until the front of his jacket grazed my chest. I saw his hand rise until it touched my shoulder and slowly traced a line down my arm. My breath caught in my throat, and my eyes slammed shut. Paralyzed by what was sure to follow, I stood there, my mind warring with my heart. "Do this?" I felt the faint graze of his lips on my cheek.

A flash of familiarity shot through me, jarring me from the moment. I took a step back and stared up at Fenris. His playful expression was gone altogether. In its place was a hopefulness I hadn't expected to see. One that didn't seem related to his eagerness to kiss me.

"Good night, Fenris."

His expression fell for a moment, but he righted it with a smirk and a mischievous stare.

"Good night, Eve." He walked back to the door and opened it. "Please call me if you need me."

"I will."

He hovered for a moment, looking at me like he was trying to read between the lines of my expression. Judging by the furrow of his brow, he hadn't succeeded.

"I'll see you around, Eve."

He stepped out into the hall and disappeared down the steps. I locked my apartment and walked to the front window to watch him get into his car. He stopped in the middle of the street and looked up, his expression still pensive, but he waved when he saw me, his eyes brightening the second they landed on me.

Then he got into his car and drove away.

I couldn't understand why that made me feel so empty,

why his leaving bothered me like it did. He'd offered to stay—if I hadn't wanted him to leave, then why had I pushed him out? My conflicting feelings were starting to hurt my head, so I went into the bathroom and got ready for bed, hoping sleep would solve my problems for me.

But since sleep barely came, it never really had a chance.

16

——∈《《·•·》》∋——

I woke up after a couple of hours of interrupted sleep feeling mostly human. I didn't know what the other part was, but I knew it wasn't good. Something half-dead. If I didn't get an actual night's sleep soon, it wasn't going to be pretty—for anyone.

As I dragged myself to the kitchen to make coffee, I heard my phone vibrating with an incoming call. I picked it up to find my least favorite student advisor calling.

"Yeah," I grunted.

"We need to meet," Iver said, as if that were explanation enough.

"Why?"

"To make sure you're on the right path, remember?"

"It's about the same as the last time I saw you. No need to meet up."

Silence.

"I'll see you tomorrow at eleven a.m. Don't be late. I don't have time for games."

He hung up before I could deliver my sluggish-but-snappy retort.

"Asshole," I said, tossing my phone onto the counter. I made my way into the living room and plopped down on the couch to wait for the coffee. With my head rested back, I closed my eyes. In the haze between wake and sleep (which I currently lived in), I saw something—or someone. He stalked toward the forefront of my mind through a literal fog. I could see his silhouette but not his face. With every step he took, I could feel my chest tighten. Slowly, he grew nearer until he was so close that his features began to come clear. Like my blurry vision was starting to focus. He leaned toward me, his eyes breaking through the fog. They were black and angry and familiar, and I shot up on my couch screaming.

My heart was racing in my chest, and I ran into the kitchen to the drawer where I'd stuffed Stian's sketch away. Sure enough, I saw those same eyes staring back at me. Haunting me.

With shaking hands, I poured myself a carafe of coffee, thinking a shit-ton of caffeine was warranted. I spilled some on the counter, and when I grabbed a towel to wipe it up, I realized it was cold. Then I looked up at the window and realized it was dark outside.

"What the fuck...?" I muttered under my breath as I reached for my phone. I looked at the time, and my eyes nearly bugged out of my face. "Shit!" I yelled. It was nine p.m. "How did that happen?"

I knew I was tired, but that was ridiculous. I'd literally slept the day away.

I checked my messages. Two calls from Charlie, asking where I was—I'd missed my TA class—and one from Fenris, making sure everything was okay. His call had come only an hour earlier. I wondered if he'd be by to check on me if I didn't call him back. As much as I enjoyed being around him—and how easy it was to forget everything going on around me with him there—I wasn't up for his earnest interrogation. I knew he would want to dig, and I couldn't deal with it. I wanted to be left alone, but not to actually *be* alone.

I was still a bit riled by my dream.

I decided to get cleaned up and go out—an alcohol-free night, for once. An hour later, I made my way to the coffee shop just off the northwest corner of campus and got a cup of chamomile tea to help calm me down. It was late, but the place was packed full of hipsters and wannabe philosophers discussing everything from music to politics. Sometimes a combination of music and politics. I slumped down in my booth and played around on my phone, trying to drown out their conversations.

Until something—or someone—else proved a better distraction.

"Latte girl has turned to the dark side," Stian said, sitting down across from me uninvited. The amusement in his eyes as he looked from my cup of tea to me was unmistakable. "Coffee beans all over the world are crying at this news."

"It's ten o'clock, Stian. Caffeine is bad for me after seven."

"Then what brings you here at this anti-caffeine hour? No raging party to attend? No friend to bail on at the bar?"

"About that—" I started before he cut me off with a wave of his hand.

"The bartender explained. No need to apologize. Perhaps I owe you one for leaving you alone and vulnerable to the circling vultures at that place."

"I really am sorry," I said, averting my eyes for a moment.

"I can see that," he replied with a sly smile. "Now, are

you going to answer my question and tell me what brought you here tonight?"

I held up my mug, then took a sip. "Tea." He looked unimpressed. "Pretty wild, right?"

"Positively scandalous."

"You should be careful," I warned. "You don't want to get caught up in this madness."

His smile spread. "Oh, I don't know about that," he replied, leaning forward to prop his elbows on the table. "Maybe that's exactly what I need." He took the mug from my hand and chugged its contents before returning it to me —empty. "You know, we never did finish your astrology lesson the other day. Should we do that now?"

I looked down at my empty mug and shrugged.

"You kinda killed plan A for me, so..."

"Excellent!" he said, jumping up from the booth. "I have the perfect idea, if you're up for a little more excitement than your cup of tea."

His eyes narrowed at me in challenge, and I took the bait without thought.

"Bring it, violin boy."

He quirked a brow at me. "I think you mean violin *man*, because I can assure you, there is nothing boyish about me."

With that, he turned and made his way toward the exit, never looking back. I followed with a sense of anxious exhilaration that I'd never felt before. He was waiting for me at the corner, headed toward campus. When I stopped at his side, ready to cross, he reached down and took my hand in his.

"Last chance to back out," he said with a smile. But there was a shadow behind his eyes—a sadness lingering there when he spoke. I started to ask him what was wrong, but the light changed, and he led me across the road toward the

Whitman Observatory. "I think you'll find my explanation of the constellations much more entertaining than that horrid professor's. It's shocking that the man is paid to teach anything at all. I've seen corpses more animated than he was."

"Corpses?" I asked, slipping my hand from his.

He stopped and looked at me, an apologetic expression on his face.

"Poor choice of words," he said. "I apologize. I was just trying to illustrate how awful the man is at his job. I mean, really, it's a wonder any of his students are conscious while he lectures."

He had a point. It was why I rarely went to that class.

"So just to be clear, you're not some zodiac serial killer luring me to my death, right?"

"Well that wouldn't be terribly original of me, given that there already was a zodiac serial killer..." I slapped his arm, and he laughed. "And it's not like I'd admit it if I was. Looks like you're just going to have to trust me." His expression sobered. "Can you do that? Can you trust me?"

He reached for my hand yet again and took a step closer. Something about standing out there with him under the star-filled sky felt right. I felt calm and carefree in a way that I hadn't before. Whenever I tried to entertain the idea that he might harm me, my brain rejected it immediately, as though it literally could not process that thought.

I took a deep breath and let it out slowly. "I think I can."

He smiled down at me. "Then let's go."

※

"WHAT IN THE hell are you doing?" I asked Stian as he pulled a tiny case out of his pocket. He opened it up to

Eve of Eternal Night

reveal little metal tools, the kind I'd seen burglars and detectives use in the movies to pick locks. "Are you going to break into the observatory?" My voice was a little too high-pitched to pretend I wasn't freaked out. I was all for living on the edge, but committing crimes—I tried to shy away from that, if for no other reason than to avoid my father's wrath. I'd incurred it once. I was in no hurry to relive that experience.

"Don't worry. They don't have cameras in the building. Nobody will know we've been here."

"Do they have alarms? Because that'll sure as hell let someone know we're here if we trip one."

He looked over his shoulder at me and smiled. "You're cute when you worry."

"Totally my goal," I deadpanned. "To be criminal eye candy."

"You're only a criminal if you get caught," he said just as I heard a light click of the lock. His smile widened. "After you..."

He pushed the door open, revealing a vast room with a massive telescope angled at the windowed wall. The view through the transparent wall was stunning enough, but Stian wasn't satisfied with that. He took me by the hand and led me over to the huge telescope worth God only knew how much. He leaned down to look through it, then started to jimmy with its buttons and levers, making it move.

"Oh my God! Don't touch it! What if you break something?"

"I won't," he said, sounding way too confident for my liking. "Here." He stepped away so that I could move toward the mammoth telescope. "Put your eye here and look. I want you to see this."

I did as he asked, doing my best to not actually touch anything and leave DNA on it—just in case. The radiance of the stars that I gazed upon was unlike anything I'd ever seen. My hand drifted up as if to touch what was light years away. Stian captured that hand and held it captive.

"Do you know what you're looking at?"

"No," I replied, keeping my snarky comeback of 'stars' to myself.

"That's Gemini."

"Okay..." His lack of further explanation led to an awkward silence between us. "What's the deal with Gemini? Is it another one of those portal thingies you're big on?"

"I don't know. What do *you* think?"

I pulled away from the telescope to assess his expression. He sounded wistful again—like he had the day he'd crashed my astronomy class—and I couldn't ignore it. Just like that day, there was a faraway look in his eyes as he stared out the window at the constellation in question. This time, I could see the taint of sadness on his face.

"Stian," I said, stepping toward him. "I want to know what *you* think when you see Gemini."

He looked down at me, eyes so full of emotion that I could barely hold his stare. "I see unparalleled beauty and strength."

His gaze didn't waver as he stepped closer to me, our bodies only inches apart. I felt his hand brush my arm as he reached for my face, the light of the moon pouring in through the windows to highlight his profile. The sharp angles were softened by it somehow—or maybe it was how he was looking at me. Either way, I couldn't break my gaze. He looked like a celestial being, and it made me wonder if he didn't truly belong somewhere up in the sky, surrounded by the constellations he held so dear.

"Do you see those things when you look at her?" he asked, his voice husky and low.

"At who?"

"At *Gemini*."

"I just see stars," I said. My reply sounded like an apology.

"Such a pity," he said, leaning closer still. "There's so much more to her than that."

I stood unmoving as his face neared mine. His eyes fell to my lips, and they parted instinctively, letting loose my bated breath. There was something magnetic about Stian in that moment that I hadn't seen before. A beauty and strength of his own, brought out by the starry sky above. I wanted to be swept up in his cosmic glory.

His breath on my cheek caused my eyes to roll closed as I awaited his contact. Then the sound of a door crashing open startled them open.

"How did you two get in here?" a man shouted. I spun around to find my professor glaring at us. "Someone had better start talking, or I'm calling campus security."

"I'm so sorry, sir," I said, grabbing my purse off the ground. "We're leaving."

"Oh no you're not. I need your name, young lady. His, too."

"Eve Carmichael." His expression sobered for a moment before his anger returned.

"And you, young man?"

Stian laughed. "Stian."

"Last name."

"It's just Stian. Like Sting. No last name necessary."

"Okay," my professor said, reaching for his cell phone. "If you want to get cute with me, we'll do it the hard way."

"C'mon Eve," Stian said, taking my hand in his. "Let's go."

"You'll stay right where you are," the professor countered. Stian walked right up to him, all humor erased from his expression. Left in its wake were harsh shadows and an anger that made me want to retreat.

"No," he said, "we won't." Then he stormed past the middle-aged man without so much as a glance in his direction, dragging me behind him.

"The dean will be hearing about this!"

"Stian," I said, spitting out his name like a curse. "I'm going to be in so much shit!"

"You'll be fine. You needed to do this," he replied, still hauling me toward the staircase.

"I *needed* to see a constellation so badly that I'm going to end up on some kind of probation?"

He stopped short, and I nearly slammed right into him. That same hard expression was on his face as he stared down at me.

"*Yes.*"

A flash of light coming from down the hall got our attention, along with the unmistakable sound of a walkie-talkie. Security was on its way, which was not going to improve things if they caught us. Mad at Stian or not, I followed him as he bolted down the stairs. By the time we hit the first floor, we were in an all-out sprint across the common. I was angled toward my apartment. Stian, however, was headed toward the south side of campus.

"See you tomorrow, latte girl!" he shouted, laughing.

"I'm going to kill you!" I replied, letting out a little laugh of my own. Yeah, I was pissed that we'd gotten busted, but I wasn't really mad at him. If I had it to do over again, I would. Sharing that moment with him in the observatory had been well worth it.

Even more worth it if we hadn't been interrupted.

Eve of Eternal Night

I AWOKE to the phone call I'd been expecting. Sarah at the dean's office was the first line of offense in what promised to be an epic meeting with the big cheese himself. She made it clear that I was to go there immediately, and that I was lucky that charges weren't being pressed. I had to fight hard to swallow down my retort—something about my father and his legal team and being buried in paperwork and motions for the rest of her life—but I managed to keep it in. Maybe there had been a time when I wouldn't have, but in reality, I was in the wrong, and I knew it. Maybe contrition would go a long way with the dean.

Then again, maybe it wouldn't.

After my stern warning was completed, I hung up the phone and got dressed. A few minutes of getting cleaned up in the bathroom and a bagel later, I was out the door, doing my walk of shame to see the dean. I wondered if he'd called Iver to meet me there, too. A double team of cold stares and animosity was exactly what I didn't need. Iver would find out soon enough, no doubt—probably before our scheduled meeting. The man had a gift for digging up dirt.

I walked through the main building to the dean's office, meeting Sarah's scowl with a bitchy smile. I'd vowed to be contrite with the dean, not his minion. She pointed toward his door as though I wasn't well acquainted with its location, and I blew right past her. I wanted to get our meeting over with. Whatever I had to say or do to get out of there was the order of the morning.

"Breaking and entering is a felony, Ms. Carmichael," the dean said by way of greeting.

"Only if your intent was to commit a felony once inside," I replied, dropping my bag next to my usual chair and sitting down. "I didn't touch anything in that room, and I had no intention—or means, for that matter—of stealing your über expensive telescope."

He scowled at me, and I realized my mission to get out of there as quickly as possible was already fucked.

"Semantics aside, you committed a crime on my campus last night."

"Technically, I didn't commit it. Someone else did. I just happened to be there."

"Aiding and abetting is still a crime."

"I was just a bystander. No aiding and abetting for me."

His irritation was evident in his creased brow. I was trying his already thin patience by the look of it.

"So you had an accomplice," he said, pushing his seat back to stand up. He walked around his desk and stopped in front of me. He hovered there, trying to assert his dominance over me—a weak attempt to intimidate the girl raised by the most vicious lawyer on the eastern seaboard.

"That implies I was involved, so no, I didn't. There was someone else there. Professor what's-his-name knew that, though, so I'm assuming you do too."

"His name?"

"You should know that as well."

"All Professor *Smith* told me was the culprit's first name, and it appears to be a false one."

"I don't know his last name, and his first is the one I know him by, so I can't help you with that."

"How do you know him?" he asked, taking a step back to better assess my reaction. I, of course, gave him nothing.

"From around campus."

The dean's grim expression slowly morphed into one of pure delight. Delight at something I couldn't figure out, which made me nervous. I prided myself on being a step ahead of him at every turn. This disadvantage was troubling. I knew his elation at my admission couldn't be a good sign.

"That's interesting, Eve, because Sarah spent the better part of the morning searching for a 'Stian' in our records, and it seems that there is no student, currently enrolled or otherwise, by that name. First, middle, or last." When his smile widened, I knew the shock I felt at his words had bled into my expression. "So I'll ask you once more, Ms. Carmichael. How do you know this individual?"

"I'm telling the truth! I've seen him around campus. He's usually in the common, playing his violin or lounging around reading a book."

"Have you ever seen him coming or going from class?"

"Well no, but I just figured he's a slacker. Wouldn't be the only one on this campus."

"No. Not with you here."

"Listen, I don't want to sit around and argue about who he is or isn't. I don't know the answers, okay? Can I go now?"

"If you'd like to be the one I report to the police about the break-in, then yes. Feel free to leave."

"You and I both know you're not going to do that, for obvious reasons."

He assessed me for a moment before stepping back to lean against his desk.

"Maybe you're right. Maybe I'm bluffing. But you should ask yourself something, Eve. Ask yourself what kind of element you're consorting with these days." He laughed, letting his head fall back a bit before pinning his beady eyes back on mine. "I mean, you're not even sure you know his real name. How long have you known him?"

I shrugged. "Maybe a week or two—"

"How long before that do you remember seeing him

around campus?" I paused, considering his question for a moment. I didn't like the conclusion I came to. In all my time at that school, I couldn't recall having seen Stian's face before the day I met him in the common. Before he wriggled his way into my life. "I'm assuming by your sudden pallor that it wasn't long before you became involved with him."

"No," I said softly.

"And yet you're now on the hook for a crime because of him."

"I... I just..."

"You just what, Ms. Carmichael? Were so desperate for someone to like you that you suspended all common sense so you could have a friend? So you let someone into your life without knowing the first thing about him?" *Yes.* That was the sad but true answer to his rhetorical question. "Do you even have a way to reach him?" I shook my head, unable to talk without my feelings betraying me. Just like Stian had. "I am going to let you go today, Ms. Carmichael, because I don't believe that you were the brains behind the break-in, and I don't really want to have to deal with your father if I don't need to. Nothing was stolen or damaged; no need to blemish your record any more than you already have. But hear me when I say this, young lady: you need to be careful whom you consort with. You might find yourself in a situation that even your father can't get you out of."

I nodded again, picking up my bag as I rose from my chair. My dismissal was plain in his tone. I turned and walked to the door, trying not to hang my head in shame like I wanted to. Though I was loath to admit it, he was right. About all of it. Whatever freedom I felt around Stian—whatever effect he had on me—would only lead to something bad. That much was clear. I needed to distance myself from him.

My phone vibrated in my pocket as I walked down the hall, but I ignored it, the dean's words still echoing through my mind with every step I took. I let them permeate my brain, soaking in until I accepted them as fact. Stian was trouble, plain and simple. And that was my best-case scenario.

As my mind wandered down a dark road, forcing pieces of a puzzle together, I wondered if Stian's presence in my life was about something else entirely. Something far more sinister. He'd mysteriously shown up the day after I'd witnessed the murder on Greek Row, and according to the dean, he wasn't even a student at the college. So why hang out there, and why take such a keen interest in me? I could only think of two reasons. Maybe three.

One: my father. Two: the tabloids. Three: someone with a vested interest in finding out what I knew about that night —like someone involved in the crime itself. He'd also been at the Sketchy Fox the night I saw the murder in the alcove.

My blood ran cold at the thought.

I quickened my pace and burst through the exit that faced the common. I scanned the grassy area, searching for the man in question. It wasn't long before my eyes fell upon him, leaning against his usual tree. His eyes met mine across the vast space, and my breath caught in my throat.

Without thinking, I turned the other way and headed for the perimeter of campus. It was the long way to get to my office, but it would keep me from encountering Stian. To say I was now suspicious of him would be an understatement. To say I feared him a little would be far more accurate.

What-ifs started to rattle around in my head as my thoughts spiraled downward. By the time I reached the chemistry building, I was on the verge of a panic attack. I ran down the hall to my office and slammed the door behind me, locking it. I leaned my back against it and slid down, doing everything I could to calm my breathing. My vision started to narrow and darken, and I lay down for fear I would pass out like last time and hurt myself.

I got out my phone and the scrap of paper with Gunnar's cell number on it, then tried to focus on the numbers. They narrowed with every breath I took, but I managed to read them and punch them into my new phone. I hit 'talk' and held it to my ear while I fought for breath.

"Eve?" he said, concern in his voice. "Is everything all right?" My lack of response did little to assuage that concern. "Eve, where are you? I need you to tell me." I opened my mouth and tried to force words out, but little more than a screechy, strangled sound escaped. Gunnar started listing off potential places I could be, listening for a cue from me to confirm his guess. When he landed on my office, I managed to make one of those pitiful sounds again. "I'll be right there. Stay on the line with me."

I could hear him running, his heavy footfalls echoing through the phone. A small part of me started to calm, knowing he was coming for me. That he would find me, even if what he found was a train wreck of a girl lying on the dirty concrete floor of her office. There was comfort in knowing he cared enough to come at all. That he was invested in my well-being.

Even if it was a lost cause.

He kept talking to me as he ran, his breath coming in ragged gasps between sentences. I couldn't get myself to reply, but his words kept me on the right side of falling. I started to come back from the ledge I was balanced on, the elephant on my chest slowly retreating.

Eve of Eternal Night

What seemed like an eternity later, the door at my back started to shake as Gunnar pounded on it, calling my name. After two attempts, I managed to push myself up far enough to unlock the door. It bumped me when he threw it open, his head poking around the corner to see me looking like a hot disaster on the floor.

His sigh of relief at the sight of me was duly noted.

He didn't say anything at first. Instead, he maneuvered his way into the room and closed the door before crouching down beside me to take my face in his hands. He tilted it up to catch the light, looking into my eyes one at a time. Then he reached down to my wrist to take my pulse. Once he seemed satisfied that I was alive and breathing, he spoke.

"You gave me quite a scare there, Eve."

I had to clear my throat twice before I could reply. "Panic attack..."

He nodded in understanding. "Those can be terrifying."

"An accurate assessment," I joked, straightening my spine against the door.

"Was there a particular trigger? Do you want to talk about it?"

"I could use some water first," I said, pointing to where I'd thrown my bag. He unclipped my water bottle from it and handed it to me. After a few big sips, my throat felt better. "Thanks."

"No problem."

"No... I mean for everything. For coming..."

His expression softened as he sat down next to me.

"I gave you my number for a reason."

"Because you knew I was a time bomb waiting to go off?"

He laughed at my morbid assessment. "No, Eve. I gave it to you because I wanted to help you—to be there if you ever needed something."

"Looks like I needed something."

"So do you want to talk about it?"

I shook my head. "Not really, but I probably should." He looked at me, his keen eyes assessing my demeanor. Always observing. "It's a long story, but the short of it is that I may or may not have been with someone who broke into the observatory last night. We got caught and ran. The dean called me in this morning and grilled me on what happened, threatening to press charges if I didn't give up the guy I was with.

"He already knew his first name, and I didn't know his last, so even if I'd wanted to, I couldn't have told him. The dean backed me into a corner and then made me look stupid when he told me that the guy—who I've been hanging out with—isn't even a student here. That I don't know the first thing about him."

"That must have been upsetting."

"It was, but not for the reasons you're thinking." I looked away from him, picking at a divot in the lid of my water bottle. "Aside from being made to feel like a complete idiot, the dean made me realize that this guy seemed to magically appear the day after the party when I saw—"

Gunnar looked at me expectantly.

"Yes?"

"When I thought I saw that murder. So now I have this super weird guy hanging around, trying to get close to me. Don't you think that's a bit odd?"

"Could be a coincidence."

"Or it could be something entirely different. He doesn't go to school here. He's not a student. He's just some random dude who keeps running into me."

"You think he's related to that event somehow?"

"I think that's a pretty decent likelihood, don't you?

What better way to find out what I know about that night than to get close to me and get the info from me? I'm too high profile to mess with in any other way. And though he could be some tabloid asshole trying to get compromising pics of me—*again*—I just don't get that vibe. But something is off about him. I'm just mad I didn't see it before."

"You thought he liked you...?" His question was gentle, but it still stung.

"Yes."

We sat there in silence for a moment before Gunnar stood up, reaching a hand out to me. I looked at it and then at him.

"It's just a gesture of help, Eve. It's okay to need help sometimes. We all do."

With a sigh, I took what he offered.

Once he hauled me up, I brushed the dirt off my jeans and straightened out my clothes. A swipe of my fingers under my eyes to wipe away the mascara undoubtedly smudged there, and I was good to go. At least physically speaking.

"What now, doc?"

He feigned anger at my use of that title. "That depends on you. What would you like to do? We could go back to my office and talk more about this."

"Or," I started, acting like I was about to offer the best idea ever, "we could forget this whole thing ever happened."

"We don't have to talk about it, but I can't pretend that it didn't happen. And I don't think that you should, either. If you ever want to work past your issues, you will have to face this eventually."

"But how do I face the fact that I may or may not have some killer following me around campus? How do we therapy that one away?"

His calm expression darkened for a moment before returning, like a passing shadow had befallen his face only to disappear.

"*We* can't," he replied, emphasizing the 'we'.

"Calling the cops isn't an option. I have nothing to report to them."

"I know. The police aren't the answer. Neither is the dean."

"Which brings us back to square one."

"Not exactly."

"No, really, it kinda does."

"Did you see him today?"

"Yeah, right before I ran over here and flipped out."

"Describe him to me." I did as he asked and gave him Stian's description and likely whereabouts, providing he hadn't bailed when I took off running. When I finished, Gunnar didn't say a word. Instead, he opened the door to my office and stepped through it.

"So now what?" I asked.

He looked over his shoulder at me and smiled. "I've got a few minutes before my next appointment. I thought I might go for a stroll around the common."

"Gunnar—"

"Eve, do me a favor and stay here. Keep your door locked. And call me if anyone comes by, okay?"

"Okay, but what are you going to do? Like *really* do?"

"I'm going to go have a little chat with the campus loiterer."

"Do you think that's a good—"

"I think I'm ex-military and can handle myself just fine, Eve. I won't make things worse for you, I promise." I stared at him, skepticism plain in my eyes. His eyes narrowed in response. "Do you trust me?"

In a clinical sense, or...?

"Yes. I trust you."

"Then do as I asked and stay here until you hear from me, okay?" I nodded in response. "Good. I'll message you shortly."

He pulled the door shut behind him without another word, and I locked it just as he'd instructed. My feet carried me back to my desk, and I plopped down in my chair. I stared at the door Gunnar had just exited through, wondering what crazy-ass thing he was about to do. I had zero doubts that Gunnar could handle himself; his build alone spoke to that. But I couldn't help but wonder what the hell his game plan was. How he was going to make my little problem go away. Because even if he succeeded in making Stian leave me alone, I highly doubted he'd get any answers from him regarding why he was cozying up to me. No criminal would give that up, no matter how ex-military Gunnar was. Unless he was special ops and well versed in torture—then he might be able to make Stian talk. But there was no evidence to support that theory, so torturing the truth out of Stian probably wasn't going to happen.

Not that I wanted it to.

A traitorous part of my body cringed at the thought of harm coming to him. That sad little part that was as desperate for friendship as the dean had said. I wanted to rip that part out and stomp on it a few times. It needed to be taught a lesson—or reminded of one, in case it had forgotten. Letting people in ended badly.

Always.

17

I waited in my office for a call from Gunnar, but twenty minutes later, an appointment reminder on my phone beeped, alerting me that I needed to get over to Iver's office. Tempting though it was to bail, I had a sneaking suspicion that avoiding him just wasn't a thing. That he'd show up on my doorstep if he had to, and I wanted to avoid that like the plague.

After a few cleansing breaths, I made my way over to his office. The door was closed, but I could hear him talking to someone. Actually, it bordered on shouting. He was pissed about something, that much was clear.

I stood outside his closed office door and listened from my side of the glass-paned divider. He sounded so angry. I pressed closer, eavesdropping on his one-sided conversation.

"I'm aware that there's a problem," he said, doing nothing to hide his irritation. I could see his large silhouette stalk across his tiny office, phone in hand. "I know that, too. What I don't know is what you expect me to do about it. I can't control her any more than you can." Silence. "You want me to force her somehow? That's an interesting plan. How exactly would you like me to accomplish that, hmm? Kidnap her? Take her hostage and interrogate her to see what she's figured out, if anything?" More silence. I could practically hear Iver seething through the door. "You know this has to be handled delicately. It always does. One wrong step and everything is lost." The hair on the back of my neck started to stand on end, as if my survival instincts were aware of something my mind had yet to comprehend. As if my limbic system were begging me to get the hell out of there. But there I stayed. "If Stian burned his bridge, then I'll fix it. I always do. Eve will get on board as soon as possible. She has no other option. We're running out of time."

Peeking through the corner of the window so as not to be seen, I watched as Iver lowered his arm and tossed his phone onto his desk. Then I heard a crash against the wall that shook the door I was spying through. I took off running out of the advisors' main office and down the hall. I didn't care how crazy I looked, I just needed to get away. Away from what, was the question.

I took a shortcut between buildings to get to the student union, which was always full of people. In that moment, I wanted to be in a crowded room. I feared my life depended on it.

I practically dove into a cushy chair near a window, earning me stares from a few passers-by, but I didn't give a shit. They could stare all they wanted. I had some cryptic BS to figure out and fast. Overhearing Iver's conversation had made a few things clear to me. First, he was far from on my team like he pretended to be. Second, he and Stian were in cahoots, which was ominous at best. Whatever they were up to, they were in it together—I just had to figure out what it was.

That thought made me question the other newcomers to my life. Gunnar had done nothing but help me—even with the Stian situation. Iver had suggested I see him, but was that enough to suspect him? I just wasn't sure. Had it been the other way around, then yes. But it wasn't.

I'd technically met Fenris before the murder I was convinced I'd seen in Greek Row, but he'd been so eager to get close to me that night that I should have kept my guard up. I hadn't, even though I knew better than to let it down. Something about him just made me want to.

He remained a question mark for the time being.

I pulled out a notebook and started jotting down the bits of the conversation I'd overheard outside Iver's office, writing the points down in bullet form. When I looked the half-full page over, nothing about it was comforting. No matter how paranoid I thought I was becoming, that conversation was a bad omen. 'Kidnap' and 'interrogate' were ominous at best.

I knew my father wasn't involved in whatever was happening. He might have sent one spy, but he wouldn't have amassed a team of them. That left tabloids or the killers as potential options, both terrible ones for very different reasons. In the past, dubious 'news' sources had used sketchy means to get close to me to gain information on my parents. Over time, I'd gotten better at picking them out, so they'd been forced to find more insidious ways of infiltrating my non-existent inner circle. If that was indeed what Stian and Iver were working to do, they'd done it in a far more effective way than any of the others ever had. It would explain why Iver knew so much about me—so much more than your average advisor—as well as his age. Yes, he was technically old enough for his position, but barely. And he certainly didn't seem like he enjoyed it very much. The

Eve of Eternal Night

dean seemed awfully supportive of him as well, which made me even more suspicious. The dean would love an opportunity to besmirch my family name in the press. He wouldn't care which Carmichael was on the receiving end.

That theory seemed to make more and more sense as I scribbled notes along the margins of my list, drawing wild lines to connect my thoughts on paper. When I was satisfied I'd thought that possibility through, I sat back and reread the original conversation. It all lined up until I got to the very end. Why would they be running out of time? Tabloids wouldn't have a deadline to meet—not for a salacious story involving a family as famous as mine. So why would time be such a pressing matter? And why would Iver think he had a way to win me over where Stian had failed?

And if the dean was involved, why would he have given Stian up?

I turned the page and titled it "killers."

At first, it seemed a stretch, but as I continued to jot down what I knew, I wasn't so sure that was the case. Stian and Iver both had the size and build to have been among the five I'd seen that night between the buildings. And I knew they were working together, which would make sense as well. If they'd recognized me, maybe they were just trying to see what I knew. Iver had said something about kidnapping me to see what I knew, but at the time, I'd thought he was being sarcastic. But what if he wasn't? What if he was as serious about that as he seemed to be about everything else?

Shit.

As my hands grew clammy, I realized something else that was worrisome. Something I hadn't put together until that moment. If Iver and Stian were working together, then there was clearly a third party involved; the person on the other end of that call.

My murderer theory was starting to gain more traction.

I needed to know who the mystery caller was.

The buzzing cell phone in my pocket startled me, and I stifled a scream with my hand as I jumped in my seat. I fished it out and looked to see who it was, expecting Gunnar's name to flash on the screen. Instead, I saw Iver's.

I panicked, not sure what to do. I knew I couldn't avoid him forever, so I tried to steady my nerves, then hit 'talk'.

"Hello?"

"I believe we were supposed to meet today," Iver said, not bothering to greet me. "Fifteen minutes ago, to be exact."

"Something came up," I said, trying to keep my voice steady.

"Meet me here in ten."

"No can do. I have to be somewhere."

"Where?" he asked, his anger barely restrained.

"Somewhere off campus."

"You can't blow off our meeting, Eve. I have to report back to the dean, and I will not lie for you."

"Yeah, I know that. I'll... um... come in next week or something. Will that work?" I heard a door close on his end of the line, his heavy footsteps as he left his office. Was he coming to look for me? "Listen, I have to go. I'll call and schedule something later."

I hung up without another word, then gathered my things. I bolted from the student union and kept running until I was well off campus, not sure where I was headed. I eventually ended up at the Sketchy Fox.

It was the middle of the day, but the stools along the bar were almost full. I found one at the far end and sat down, dropping my backpack to the floor. To my surprise, Cheryl was already at work. I wondered if she was pulling a double.

Then I realized I didn't care why. I knew Cheryl would have my back if Stian—or anyone else trying to come after me—showed up.

"I didn't think I'd see you back here after how you left last time," she said, shooting me a glance as she grabbed a tumbler off the stack. "You ran out of here in a hurry."

"Yeah…"

"I told you that you couldn't handle him."

"That you did," I said under my breath. "He's not here, is he?"

She shook her head. "Nah. You're safe for now."

Safe for now… what a loaded sentiment that was.

She poured me a double then walked away, leaving me alone with my frayed nerves and frazzled mind.

※

A FEW HOURS and a heavy buzz later, I made my way out of the bar. I didn't want to hang out long enough for the rocker god to show up and undo me any further. I walked for a while, letting the cool air clear my mind. It wasn't yet dark, so I had a false sense of security. The light did that for a person—let them think that nothing bad could happen. But I knew that wasn't the truth.

The farther I walked, the more convinced of it I became.

I kept seeing things move at the edges of my vision; an animated drunken haze of sorts. Every time I turned to see what was there, I saw nothing. I picked up my pace to the main street, then caught a cab. The driver asked where I wanted to go, and I paused, not really sure of the answer. I didn't want to go to campus, and I certainly wasn't ready to go home yet. Iver had called three times while I was at the bar. I wondered if he'd already gone to my apartment looking for me.

I shuddered at the thought.

The driver asked again, probably wondering if I hadn't heard him. I looked up to find his nearly black eyes staring back at me in the rearview mirror. A flash of cold shot down my spine, and before I knew what I was doing, I was out of the cab and running down the street toward my father's house. It was two miles away, but there was no way in hell I was getting in another cab. The fear I felt but didn't fully understand wouldn't allow that.

Those eyes... they were the same as the ones I'd seen that night down the street from the Sketchy Fox. But there was something about them that niggled at my tequila-soaked mind. Something so familiar and ominous. Something I knew I'd seen long before the killer in the alcove had fucked with my head.

And so I ran until my pores sweat alcohol and I threw up what was left in my stomach. I felt instantly better, but with that cleansing came a slap of reality. I knew exactly where I'd seen those eyes before.

I also knew why I was running to my father's home.

When I arrived, I unlocked the back door and slipped into the kitchen. Once I'd punched in the alarm code, I made my way upstairs to where my bedroom had once been. The second I'd left for college, Nancy, his pretty new wife, had torn it apart in preparation for the baby. My room became a nursery for their love child. The metaphor wasn't lost on me. My dad's remove-and-replace M.O. was still in effect.

My belongings had been tucked away in the attic, so that's where I headed. The dust was thick in the air as I shuffled boxes around until I found a few simply marked "Eve's shit." There should have been more of them, but I was pretty certain Nancy had thinned out my things on my behalf. Ever the helpful little gold-digger.

I only had about forty-five minutes to find what I needed. Nancy's daily because-I-don't-need-a-job yoga class got out at six, and her walk home would only take fifteen minutes. I had no desire to run into that bitch. Only five years my senior, her attempts to play mommy to me made me homicidal. The last time we'd met, hair had gone flying. For her sake, I thought it best to avoid her at all costs.

It didn't take long to find a heavy box containing books. I rifled through them until I found what I was looking for: journals from my early therapy days. The few days before I had been so medicated I was barely conscious.

I gently laid the two notebooks in my lap and stared at them. I hadn't looked at those scribbled ramblings since I recovered, but I kept them just in case. Just in case I ever needed a reminder of how far I'd come. How strong I really was. I'd once pulled myself out of a darkness I couldn't begin to explain. If I had to, I knew I could do it again.

With a deep breath, I opened a black leather-bound book and started to read. At first, my thoughts weren't so incoherent. They were dark and disturbing, but still 'normal' enough. But as I progressed deeper into the book, the more that normal began to deteriorate in every way. My handwriting became more difficult to read. Sentence structure became a thing of the past. And there was no flow to the pages; just a flurry of words chicken-scratched at random, with deeply etched underlining and furious circles highlighting certain parts.

Most of the words had been traced over so heavily that I couldn't even read them, but one in particular stood out. It appeared on several occasions as I neared the end of the journal. It was the only thing written on the final page, in big, bold black letters.

DEMONS.

I dropped the book to the floor and tried to control my breathing. The second book was still in my lap, but I didn't dare open it. I no longer wanted to see what was inside. Instead, I took both books and stuffed them into my backpack before running out of the attic and down the stairs. I bolted out the back door to run down the alley behind the house, but I was stopped in my tracks by something unexpected.

My father.

"Eve?" he said, sounding surprised to see his own child at his home. "What are you doing here?"

"I just came to get some of my books—from the attic." I let my anger seep into the latter part of my reply. He didn't even flinch.

"You should have called."

"Why? I'm not allowed to come home without warning?"

"It's not really your home, though, is it? You have that high-end apartment near campus that I'm paying for."

I shook my head in disbelief.

"Yeah. Yeah, I guess I do have that. Was that what I got in the divorce? I didn't know you could divorce your children."

He let out an irritated sigh. "Let's not be melodramatic, shall we?" he said as he moved to walk by. "You remember what happened the last time you tried those antics with me."

"You still think that's what I was doing? That I was just acting up because you and Mom split?" He stopped and looked at me as though the answer to my question was plain. "For someone so sharp in a courtroom, you sure are fucking dumb."

Eve of Eternal Night

"I don't have time for this—"

"Oh, you do," I said, grabbing his arm. "For once in your miserable life, you're going to hear me when I talk to you." I whipped off my backpack and grabbed the black book out of it; the one that documented my spiral into darkness. "Read it," I said, slapping the book against his chest.

"I have things to do—"

"Read the fucking book, Dad!"

He assessed me for a moment before doing as I asked, though it was more placation than genuine interest. He flipped through the pages, scanning them for anything pertinent. But as he got deeper into the journal, his pace slowed and his brow furrowed. When he finished, he, like me, dropped the book as though it had burned him.

"What is that?" he asked, his tone a mix of irritation and fear.

"The journal I started after you and Mom separated—before you carted me off to Dr. Hoffman and drugged me into submission."

After a couple of deep breaths, he steadied himself and picked up the book. He thrust it back at me.

"What do you want, Eve? Money? Is that what this is about?"

"No! It's about you treating me like I'm yours—like you give a shit about me!"

"I find these attempts to get what you want exhausting. I always have. You're just like your mother—dramatic, irrational, and *unstable*." He shot a pointed look at the book in my hands as if to say 'and there's the proof...'.

Anger snaked up my spine, slow and cold and fueling the hatred I had for the man before me. The edges of my vision blurred, my focus solely on my father. My body thrummed with adrenaline, and the second he moved to walk away from me, I grabbed his arm. This time, I didn't release it. He yanked against my hold, but it was like iron.

"What is wrong with you?" he shouted.

His question was too loaded to answer. And the moment I opened my mouth to try, everything went to shit.

The black edges of my vision started to move, and suddenly, the object of my rage went flying across the yard, his head bloodied from a strike I didn't remember landing. Fear now cutting through my anger, I started to run toward him, then stopped dead. Those dark, moving edges of my vision started to converge on my father's limp form, descending upon him until he was blocked entirely. I threw out my arm and yelled for the black forms shrouding my father to go. A blast of white-blue light nearly blinded me, and I fell to the ground, hitting my head on the concrete.

I had no idea how long I'd been out, but I opened my eyes to find my father still lying on the grass, bleeding. My vision was perfectly normal, though my head felt like it was being torn apart from the inside. I crawled over to him. He was unconscious, but breathing. I tried to help him up, but the sound of Nancy shrieking from the back door startled me, and I dropped him.

"What are you doing?" she yelled, running into the yard. "What did you do?"

"I don't know," I said, backing away from him. "I don't know what happened."

She kept yelling at me, grabbing a stick from the yard and swinging it in my direction. I didn't know what else to do, so I snatched my backpack and my journal and took off running through the house and out the front door. I didn't stop until I reached my apartment four miles away. Breathing hard and scared shitless, I burst into the living room and slammed the door behind me. I slumped down against the wall and buried my head in my hands.

"Not again," I said, trying to choke back my emotions. "Please, not again..."

I could practically feel the lone pill bottle in my medicine cabinet calling to me, telling me everything would be all right if I just opened it up and swallowed a handful of them. It'd be so easy to just fall back into that comfortably numb place—the one without feeling or emotions. Without the fear of the fall. Because it wasn't the end result that frightened me the most; it was the knowledge that I was headed there and unable to stop. That was terrifying.

On shaky legs, I stood and made my way to the bathroom. I looked at my reflection before opening the cabinet door and snatching the orange bottle. I shook three pills out and swallowed them without water. The scrape of them down my throat was familiar, and oddly welcome in that moment.

I sat around for a couple of hours, just waiting for them to kick in. When they didn't, I contemplated taking another three, but I didn't. Instead, I ran to the kitchen in search of my stash of liquor, but I'd already drunk it dry. Frustrated, I settled on a trip back to the Sketchy Fox for more tequila. I grabbed my wallet and keys and fled my apartment.

Surely combining the drugs with alcohol would make the effects stronger. A foolproof plan, for certain. One likely to get me killed.

18

I found a stool at the bar and slumped into it. Cheryl took one look at me and shook her head.

"Twice in one day? Something sure has done a number on you, girl," she said, pulling out my favorite tequila. "You need another double?"

"At least," I said, leaning forward on the bar. As tired as I was, I was half tempted to put my head down on it and sleep.

She gave me my order, then hurried off to help someone else.

"Third time's the charm, I think," a familiar voice said. I turned to find Godric wedged in beside me, eyeing me tightly.

I let out a mirthless laugh. "There's nothing charmed about this—or me, for that matter."

His eyes narrowed. "I'm not so sure about that." I held his gaze until I couldn't any longer—partly because of the intensity, but mostly because singular images started to double. I grabbed my glass and took another sip. The numbness was starting to creep in. "So tell me something. Why do you look like hell?"

I choked on my drink, coughing until Cheryl brought me a glass of water and a look of warning.

"You don't want to know."

"Try me. Maybe I'm a good listener."

I looked him up and down, lingering on the tattoos winding up his throat, before speaking.

"Somehow I think your gifts lie elsewhere."

That earned me a wry smile. "Oh, they do. But I have layers. Don't be so quick to judge."

His words gave me pause.

"Yeah. Okay. You want to know my story? Buckle up, buttercup, because it's a bumpy ride."

And so I told him. My drunk/high self unleashed a whole shitstorm of truth (or what I thought to be truth) down upon him. I told him about the murder in Greek Row. About the shadows outside my place. About the attack down the street, and the weird visions, and the black eyes that haunted my dreams—whenever I actually fell asleep. I rambled on like the freight train of crazy I had started to feel like. Nothing was off limits. Not even my dad.

After my loose lips were done spilling all my secrets, he just stood there looking at me, his expression neutral, as if he were waiting for something else from me; something I couldn't even begin to understand. Godric, the bad boy, should have been running away after everything I'd said. But he wasn't.

For a second, I wondered if I'd actually said those things aloud or just thought them in my head.

"Why are you looking at me like that?" I asked, reaching for my drink. He beat me to it, snatching it out of my reach. "Hey, gimme that back!"

"How many of these have you had today?" he asked, his brow furrowed.

"Only a couple!" I replied. His brow quirked in disbelief. "I might have taken something else before I came here."

"What?" Not a question. A demand.

"None of your business."

I turned away from him, embarrassment heating my cheeks. Who the fuck was he to interrogate me about my choices? I got Cheryl's attention and flagged her over. She put a new glass in front of me, and I slammed its contents before the surly rocker could steal it.

As I turned around to tell him off, my phone started vibrating in my pocket. I looked to see who it was. *Fenris*. Not exactly the person I wanted to talk to at that moment, but if it got me away from the overbearing bad boy, I was in. I hopped off my stool and staggered a few paces before regaining my balance, then made my way down the hall to the rear of the bar. I pushed the back door open and stumbled out into the alley.

"Hello?" I said, steadying myself against the brick wall.

"Hey Eve! It's me."

"Hellllooooo *me*. Whassup?"

I tried to play off the fact that I'd slurred, but Fenris hadn't missed it.

"Are you drunk?"

"Possibly."

"Where are you? Do you want me to come meet you? I can get caught up, I promise," he said. I could practically hear him smiling through the phone.

"You're gonna have to take a fistful of pills if you wanna do that," I said, thinking myself helpful.

"Pills? Eve, where are you? You don't sound so good."

"I'm at home," I lied. "I think I'm gonna go to sleep. I'm soooooooooooooo tiiiiired."

"Yeah, that sounds like a bad idea, Eve." Fenris continued to talk to me for a minute, but I think I either blacked out a bit or fell asleep, because he was yelling at me by the time I snapped out of it, concern in his tone. "EVE?"

"Yep. Still here. Everything's fine," I said.

"No, it's not. I think you need help."

I looked down the alley at the sound of glass crunching underfoot. A man was headed toward the back entrance of the bar. A large, shadowy man who looked oddly familiar, but I couldn't quite place him because my vision was too blurred to focus on his face.

"Look! Here comes someone now! I bet he can help me," I said before giggling the way only extremely drunk and/or high people can. "Or maybe kill me..."

Just as the words left my mouth, I saw something shiny in his hand. Something that reflected the streetlight above. I stared at it, drawn in like a magpie. I took a step toward him, lowering the phone from my ear.

"I gotta go, Fenris."

I heard him yelling at me as the phone hit the ground.

The approaching man paused for a moment, the light falling on his face, highlighting the harsh planes. I squinted, trying my best to make out who it was. I took a step closer, hoping proximity would make up for my blood alcohol level. But it didn't.

Before I had the chance, the back door to the bar flew open and Godric ran out. The second he laid eyes on the man in the alley, he pulled something out from behind his back and lunged toward him. Everything happened so fast that I couldn't focus. I just stood there watching as they struggled with one another. Then one of them fell to the ground, motionless. The other hovered over the body.

My brain, in its drunken state, couldn't quite reconcile what I'd just seen.

Standing in the alley behind the Sketchy Fox stood Godric, now covered in blood, knife still in hand. Only parts of the silver blade caught the light of the moon. The rest was too drenched in blood and other bits to be seen.

My brain screamed for me to run, but my feet were glued to the ground, my body paralyzed with fear. Unlike the nights I'd thought I'd seen dead bodies lying on the ground, this time there was no mistaking what was right in front of me. A brutal crime had been committed before my eyes. And the murderer was standing in front of me.

"*Surprised*?" he asked in a somewhat amused tone. Given my state of paralysis, I didn't answer. "You shouldn't be."

"You... you..." I stammered on and on until I turned and threw up. I heaved until I had nothing left. I hoped I could purge the reality of what I'd just witnessed, but when I turned and saw him still standing there and the body still on the ground, I knew I was truly in hell.

"I *what*? Killed someone?" he asked. I nodded repeatedly, the motion clipped and jerky. "Oh come on, Eve. It's hardly the first time. Won't be the last, either." He cocked his head at me, taking a step closer. "I thought that was the attraction for you. Me being on the wrong side of the law."

"How could you... how could you just..."

"How could I just what? *Save* you?"

I shook my head, fumbling a step backward as he approached me.

He looked over at the victim, then back to me. "He deserved it. He was about to do something far worse to you, and I stopped him."

My staggering retreat continued until my back slammed into a rough wall. By the time I looked around to find a way out, he was already upon me, his body only inches from mine. He stared me down like the crazed killer he was, and I closed my eyes, wondering if he'd make it quick or if he'd torture me. Screams filling the night air around the bar were commonplace. I knew no one would come running to see what the fuss was. He'd kill me in that alley, and nobody would stop him.

I felt like a fool.

The longer my flesh remained uncut by his blade, the more anxious I grew. Eventually, my eyes flew open, needing to see what was happening. They met his, and it was then that I realized that they weren't the pale blue I remembered from the first night we'd met. They were dark—not dark—*black*. As black as night. As cold as death.

I knew those eyes. I'd seen them before—but not on him. On someone else.

I shook with panic as I thought about all the times I'd seen eyes just like his staring back at me from my nightmares—and from that alcove down the street. But unlike the ones before me, those had not been wide and full of concern.

"You fear me..." he said. There was no mistaking the disbelief in his tone.

"Of course I do, you fucking psycho! You just stabbed someone to death. And now you're going to kill me!"

At that, he took a step back. "You still don't remember..."

"*Remember?*" I asked, my voice tight and high. "Remember *what*? I don't even know you!"

His expression soured at my final words, and he closed the distance between us in a flash. I heard the clang of the knife hitting concrete right before his hands were on my waist, pulling me closer to him as he leaned against me.

"You let your fear cloud your mind, *Eve*." Hearing my name on his tongue did nothing to help the terror I felt in that moment. "You let it twist your feelings into something they're not. You mistake exhilaration for fear. That adrenaline pounding through your veins with every beat of your racing heart—it's not there because you're scared. It's because you recognize something in me that your brain can't yet comprehend." His right hand released my body and made its way to my hair, tucking a strand behind my ear in a gesture so sweet and gentle that I nearly forgot what was really going on in that alley. Who was really pressed against my body.

"Let me go," I said softly, hoping to appeal to whatever shred of humanity he still clung to. "I won't tell anyone..."

"Let you go?" he replied with a laugh. "That's not possible—not even if I wanted it to be."

His hand slid down my face to my jaw, caressing the sharp curve of it, then continued down my throat. He cupped it lightly—the barely contained strength in his grip palpable—and he leaned in toward me. By the time his lips were at my ear, I thought my heart would explode.

"Don't let this fear own you, Eve," he said, his lips grazing my ear. "You're so much more than this."

I felt his teeth clamp lightly on my earlobe and pull, teetering on the line between pleasure and pain, and I gasped. Then my mind blacked out, taking me far from that alley to a vision of darkness and blood and the wrath of a thousand gods. Standing above me, framed by the constant bursts of lightning behind him, stood an angel of death, covered in blood. He looked down at me, his expression hidden in shadow, and spoke.

"She's dead."

With a desperate gasp for air, I came back to the present, my body wrestling under the weight of my captor. The one who'd just killed in the alley. The one who'd killed me in my mind.

"This isn't real," I said, shaking my head.

"What did you see?" he asked, trying to hold me still.

"Help!" I screamed, ignoring him. "Help me!"

"Eve—"

"Help me!"

He clamped his hands down on my face to hold me still and stared into my eyes as if they held the answers to whatever questions he had. His expression tightened at whatever he found.

"I did this all for *you*—to *help* you," he said softly. "You'll have to forgive me for this later."

He bent my head forward and slammed it back against the wall. Nausea rolled in my stomach as my vision blurred and my knees weakened. I felt myself slipping toward the ground, the vision I'd just had of the man about to kill me running over and over again in my mind. The words 'she's dead' were the soundtrack to my final moments.

Then the world went dark.

The angel of death had won.

19

───◄◄⟨·•·⟩►───

I woke up in my bed with a raging headache. I tried to sit up and realized that wasn't going to happen. Not without throwing up.

"Holy shit," I grumbled, glancing sideways at my nightstand to see if my phone was there. Thankfully, it was, so I grabbed it, doing all I could not to move my head. Then a voice called out to me and scared the shit out of me. I shot up in bed to see who it was and instantly regretted it.

"You're up," Fenris said as he walked into my room.

"Bucket!" I yelled, knowing that I had no chance of making it to the bathroom.

He snatched the trashcan from under my desk and tossed it to me. I caught it without a second to spare, then puked my brains out. I felt better once I was done, but the throbbing in the back of my head persisted. My hand drifted up to it and found one hell of a bump.

"Ouch," I said, wincing in pain.

"Seems like you took one hell of a digger outside of the bar tonight," he replied, sitting down beside me on the bed. "Let me see how it's doing." I carefully turned so he could

Eve of Eternal Night

see it, the bucket of vomit still tight in my grasp. He sucked in a breath through his teeth, letting me know it looked as bad as it felt. "That's going to take a while to heal, Eve. You're lucky you didn't need stitches."

"How did I get home?" I asked, reaching to put the wastebasket of puke down. Fenris took it from me and carried it out of the room before returning.

"I'll clean that up later," he said with a smile. "As for how you got home..." He spread his arms wide and cocked his head. "Someone answered your phone and told me where you were. Told me that you were hurt."

I tried to remember what had happened, tried to figure out why there was an undercurrent of anger in his tone, but the events leading up to the massive goose egg on the back of my head were nowhere to be found.

"You weren't at the bar with me?"

"No. I was not at the bar because I was at home, trying to convince you to let me come over to your house—where you said you were."

A faint memory of our conversation drifted into my mind, and along with it, tidbits of me being drunk and stoned on prescription meds and totally out of control. I could have done without that reminder. Guilt suffused me, and I forced myself to look at him.

"I'm sorry, Fenris. I didn't mean to—"

"Scare the shit out of me? No, I'm sure you didn't mean to, but you did," he said, trying to bite back his anger. I reached for him and took his hand in mine. "I thought that—"

"*What*?" I asked. "You thought *what*?"

He pinned pain-filled eyes on me. "I thought you were going to die."

Had I really been that wasted? Was I really on the verge

of overdosing or blood alcohol poisoning or whatever the combination amounted to? I racked my brain for the answers, but came up short.

"So you came to the bar to get me? But... if I was unconscious, why wouldn't whoever answered have called an ambulance?"

He shrugged. "They just said where you were and hung up. I brought you right home because you looked okay at first—like you'd just had one too many and passed out. I didn't find the bump on your head until much later. I figured you might have a concussion, so I stayed here so I could check on you."

"Thanks for that," I said, throwing the blankets off my legs. It was then that I realized I didn't have any clothes on —just a T-shirt and undies. My eyes darted up to Fenris, who met my shocked expression with a straight face.

"Your clothes were all dirty from lying on the ground. I didn't want you to sleep in them."

"That was... thoughtful," I said, trying not to imply anything sordid had occurred. Fenris, shameful flirt that he was, had never done anything untoward before. He didn't seem the type to take advantage of an unconscious girl.

"I didn't—"

"I know you didn't. Relax," I said, cutting him off. "Could you pass me those jeans over there?" He did as I asked and tossed me the jeans hanging off the chair in the corner. "So... what now?"

"Do you remember what happened?" he asked. "How you ended up passed out in the alley?"

I sat on the edge of the bed and shimmied into my pants while Fenris did his best to focus elsewhere. But I could see his eyes dart to the flesh disappearing underneath the denim. They were full of need and disappointment.

"I remember going to the bar. I remember drinking. And that's about it."

His expression didn't change. "That's too bad."

"Maybe it's for the best," I countered. "Maybe there's a reason why I can't recall those events."

"The reason is your traumatic brain injury," he said, taking a step closer to me. "Maybe we should go get you checked out at the hospital. Make sure there isn't something else going on." He stopped in front of me and reached toward my face, letting his thumb stroke the sharp line of my cheekbone. "I'd feel terrible if anything bad happened to you."

"Worse than passing out behind a dodgy bar in a bad part of town?"

"Yes."

I smiled. "Look at you playing the role of concerned boyfriend."

"I don't want to *play* it, Eve," he said, letting that hand slide down to my neck. "I want to *be* it."

I looked on as his face lowered toward mine, eyes closing as he neared. His hand cupped the side of my neck just before his lips touched mine. His grip tightened ever so slightly, but that was all it took to trigger a barrage of memories—some from the night before, some not—that sent me into a downward spiral. Visions of the rocker in the alley, covered in blood, pressing against me. I pulled away from Fenris, breathing hard as I crashed against my headboard.

"Eve? What is it?" He reached for me, and I recoiled from his touch.

"I remember," I said, panic thick in my voice. "There was a body. I saw a man kill someone."

Fenris loomed above me until he crouched down at my side, making himself look smaller and less imposing.

"Eve—"

"No! I saw it. I saw it all, I know I did this time."

"Eve, I think maybe you should go see the doctor—"

"Don't do that!" I shouted, backing away from him until I was wedged into the corner of my bed and the wall. "Do not make me sound crazy."

"I'm not trying to. I'm just concerned about your head right now. I think maybe you were hurt worse than I thought."

"Get out," I said, my words little more than a snarl.

"Eve—"

"Get. Out!"

"Please don't—"

"GET OUT OF MY HOUSE!" I screamed those words so loudly that my eardrums crackled until everything around me sounded muffled, like I was under water.

Fenris hovered next to my bed, visibly struggling with what to do next. He didn't want to leave me alone, that much was clear. Whether that was because he thought my brain was bleeding or I'd gone fucking nuts, I didn't know. And I certainly didn't care. He'd hit a nerve that couldn't be soothed.

I'd rage until he did as I asked.

"I'm sorry I failed you, Eve," he said in a voice laden with guilt and a heavy sense of responsibility. "I'll go."

His head hung low as he turned and walked out of my room, then my apartment. The hollow sound of the door closing behind him seemed to ring out forever. I sat on my bed, trying my best to calm my breathing and clear my head, and failing miserably. I was spiraling fast, and it was well beyond my ability to stop it. I needed help from someone who understood me.

I needed Gunnar Fredrickson.

I fumbled with my cell phone until I pulled up his emergency number, and after two tries, I managed to call him. It rang and rang until I was certain it would go to voicemail, but on the fourth ring, a sleepy voice answered.

"Hello?"

"Gunnar! It's Eve."

"Eve," he said, suddenly sounding awake. "Is everything all right?"

"No. I need to see you. Now."

"I'll be at the office in fifteen minutes. We can meet in front of the building."

"Yeah. Okay. I'll be right over."

I hung up as he was asking me a question, but I didn't bother to call him back. Instead, I tried to hurry up and get dressed—as much as my throbbing head would allow—then searched for my keys. It took a while, but I finally found them hanging on the knob of my kitchen pantry. Fenris must not have known where to put them.

Walking to the med center seemed the best idea, not only because driving with a concussion wasn't recommended, but also because I had no idea where my car was. It was still dark outside, which made me question what time it was. In truth, I hadn't noticed when I'd looked at my phone; it hadn't been a top priority at the time. When I checked it as I walked across campus, I realized it was only five a.m. A small pang of guilt broke through my panic and paranoia. I'd probably scared the hell out of Gunnar with my call.

I was only a couple of minutes away from our meeting place when I started to see shadows dancing in my periphery. I knew visual disturbances were common with head injuries, but I was pretty sure that wasn't what was happening, even though I tried hard to convince myself otherwise. I started to jog the final few yards to the med center, my head pounding with every step. I was pretty sure I was going to puke again by the time I hit the parking lot, but I didn't care. Every fiber of my paranoid being was screaming at me to run.

I crested the small hill that flattened out into the back of the lot to see Gunnar standing by the front door. One look at me, wide-eyed and panting hard, and he was in a dead sprint toward me. The closer he got, the more the look on his face scared me.

"Eve!" he shouted, scooping me up in his arms and running back to the building. His pace seemed abnormally quick for a man carrying someone, which made me more anxious than I already was—if that were even possible. "What happened?"

When I didn't respond right away, he crashed through the door and slammed it shut behind him, not bothering to lock it. We were in his office seconds later, where he laid me down gently on the couch near the wall. His eyes searched my body for what I assumed were expected injuries. Then he took my pulse.

"Your heart is beating way too quickly."

"I ran here... with a head injury."

His expression hardened. "Maybe you should rest for a minute while I get you some water. Then we can start from the beginning." He turned to look over his shoulder out the window on the far wall. "I'll be right back."

He exited the room and closed the door behind him. I laid my head back and closed my eyes, letting the sense of calm I felt at knowing he would help me work through the craziness wash over me. If anyone could make sense of what was going on with me, it was Gunnar. That was his gift in life: somehow making everything okay.

The jiggle of the door handle sounded, and I opened my eyes to see Gunnar walking in with a bottle of water.

"Sorry that took so long. This was harder to find than I'd have thought." I pushed myself up to sit, resting my head in my hands for a second. Once I was confident I had my bearings, I looked up at him and took the bottle he offered. "Are you feeling better?"

"Yeah. A bit."

"You sounded pretty upset on the phone."

"I was," I replied, taking a swig from the bottle.

"Would you like to tell me what happened?"

"It's a long story."

He sat down in the chair nearest to me. "I've got time," he said with a faint smile.

I took a deep breath and did as he asked. I told him everything I remembered about the murder in the alcove, the strange run-in at my father's, my journals, and the murder and subsequent assault that led to me finding myself in my apartment with Fenris. Then I told him how I'd snapped when my memory of last night had returned and Fenris had tried to downplay it. How I was slipping down a dangerous slope again. How I feared my mind was barely hanging on.

When I was finished, Gunnar sat quietly, studying me with thoughtful eyes.

"I now understand why you were so upset when you called."

"Yeah, about that. I'm sorry I woke you—I had no clue what time it was."

"I'm always here for you, Eve. That's my job—my duty. You don't need to apologize."

I forced a quick smile before hiding my emotions behind

the water bottle, taking a long, drawn-out drink to let the awkwardness of the moment dissipate.

"So Freddie," I said, trying to lighten the mood. "What do you think?"

"I think you were assaulted and sustained a severe trauma tonight, which you are understandably shaken up about."

"But the murder—you believe me, right? That it happened?"

"What I believe isn't important, Eve—"

"It is to me! Your opinion sure as fuck matters."

He took a second to regroup before speaking. "My opinion matters to you... let's talk more about that."

"What else is there to say? I care what you think. I don't want you to see me as some damaged little girl!"

"Do you see yourself as a damaged little girl?"

Yes.

"No."

"Then why would I?"

"Don't start with all that conventional mind voodoo, Gunnar. I want you to level with me—off the record. Do you believe me? Do you believe I saw what I saw?"

He took a deep breath before standing up and walking over to sit beside me. His leg was so close that it brushed against mine, and I wondered if he did that so I'd think he was breaking the rules in that moment—that he was about to tell me the truth.

"I think someone smashed your head and you have a concussion. That much I know is true."

"But you think I'm lying about the rest?"

"I didn't say that. I can't confirm or deny what you saw because I wasn't there. I do have an idea, though—one that will require a great deal of trust on your part." He looked at

Eve of Eternal Night

me, driving his point home. "Can you do that? Can you trust me?"

He reached his hand out toward me and left it hanging in the air, waiting to see if I'd take it. I didn't have to think about it for long. The truth was, I did trust him. From almost the moment I'd met him, I'd known he was my ally. Someone who had my back. So I took the hand he offered and let him help me up from the couch.

I followed him out of the building to his car and climbed in the passenger side. He asked me again where it had all happened, and I told him. Then we were on our way. It didn't take long to see that he was taking me to the Sketchy Fox.

Gunnar parked the car not even a block from the bar. At that hour of the morning, spaces were a lot easier to come by. I spotted my car further down the street and made a mental note to make sure I drove it home when we left. I wasn't sure that mental note would hold up after we did what we were about to do, but it was the best I option I had.

"Which way?" Gunnar asked, looking at me across the roof of the car.

"It was down the back alley," I said, pointing in that direction.

He nodded once, then made his way around to the sidewalk and me. When he walked past and I didn't follow, he stopped short and turned to face me.

"It'll be okay, Eve."

My fractured mind seemed inclined to disagree.

When I remained still, he came over to me and placed his hands on my shoulders.

"I won't let anything happen to you," he said, his tone as earnest as his expression.

"You can't say things like that," I argued, looking past him to the alley awaiting us. "You're not supposed to."

His eyes softened, searching mine for something—some semblance of understanding. When he didn't find it, he exhaled hard and reached down to take my hand in his.

"I thought I told you before—I'm not your average therapist."

Before I could respond, he gently led the way over to where my nightmare had occurred. With the early light of the morning dawning on us, the space looked far less intimidating, but I was still in a full sweat by the time we reached the back of the Sketchy Fox. I stared down at the concrete in utter disbelief. It was clear from the lack of bloodstains and police tape that no crime had been committed there.

Or at least none that hadn't been quickly covered up.

"I swear it happened," I said under my breath, pulling my hand from Gunnar's to walk over to the very spot where the body had been splayed across the alley. "It was right here. And the killer—he stood over it like this. The blade was in his left hand... I remember because it was the one closest to me, and I had some morbid thought about how many left-handed murderers there were in the world..."

"Eve—"

"But then he stared at me with those wild, haunted eyes of his, and I froze. I didn't even try to run. Isn't that crazy? That I knew what he was capable of and I didn't even try to escape?"

"Maybe you knew he wasn't going to kill you," he offered.

"No. Maybe he wasn't. Maybe he likes to play with his toys before he breaks them."

I was staring off into the distance when I heard Gunnar's phone ring. I could see him in my periphery pulling it out to see who was calling. I wondered if maybe another one of his patients was also losing their shit. How inconvenient that would have been.

"You can get it," I said, giving him permission he hadn't asked for. "I'm fine."

"They can wait," he replied, taking a step closer to me. "Do you want to tell me more? Show me more?"

"You know the rest," I said, my voice weak and hollow. "I made it all up in my head..."

"Eve," he started, taking another step toward me. I snapped my wide eyes to him, and he stopped short. "Eve, I want to try something with you. Something incredibly unorthodox. Is that okay?"

"You just admitted that you don't exactly follow the therapist handbook anyway," I replied, implying permission.

"I don't want you to be afraid."

"I think we're well past that at this point."

"I wish there were an easier way to do this, Eve. I just don't see another way." I swore I heard him mumble under his breath, "we're running out of time."

"Just do it," I replied, sounding as empty as I felt. My sanity was waning with every moment I stood in that alley with him, remembering all the nuances of a crime that apparently hadn't been committed. What could he possibly do to make it worse? What possible tool of his could knock that already shaky foundation out from under me?

"I want you to meet someone," he said, taking a step closer to me. "A friend of mine."

He turned to look down toward the mouth of the alley and the figure now occupying it. The second I saw him, my knees went weak with terror. I would have screamed had I been capable of breathing, but it seemed that function had left me, along with myriad others.

Godric seemed to have that effect on me.

"Nonononononono," I said over and over again until I gasped for air.

"Eve," Gunnar said, hurrying toward me. I batted at his outstretched hand and scrambled backward away from him. I felt like such a fool. Like somehow I should have seen that coming, even though there'd been no reason to believe they knew one another. Maybe that was just my paranoia talking.

"You stay away from me," I yelled, pointing to both of them. I reached into my back pocket for my phone, but my shaking hands fumbled it to the ground. I didn't take my eyes off them as I scrambled to pick it up. Not that I could have done much if they made their move, but I wanted to be ready for it. I wanted to be ready to run.

Once I scooped my phone off the ground, I continued to back away from them. They were stalking toward me slowly but with clear intent. I needed to call for reinforcements and fast. I managed to type in 9-1-1 after three attempts and was just about to hit 'send' when I bumped into something hard behind me, dropping my phone yet again.

Out of sheer reflex, I spun around to see if I'd backed myself into a corner, silently praying that I hadn't. I turned right into a *who*, not a *what*. My eyes drifted up to see Fenris looking down at me, a mix of confusion and anger in his expression. Then he looked past me to the duo approaching, and I breathed a sigh of relief, however small. I wasn't alone. Fenris, dutiful would-be boyfriend that he was, had somehow followed me to the alley.

The rescuer I hadn't known I'd need.

"Help me," I pleaded, pulling on his shirt as I tried to drag him down the alley with me. "They're going to kill me—kill *us*."

But Fenris didn't move. Instead, he hooked his arms

Eve of Eternal Night

around me and held me in place as the others neared. Terror and betrayal like I'd never experienced in my life cut through me like a knife, gutting me alive. Whatever bizarre conspiracy was going on, I didn't understand it. All I knew in that moment was that my ass was as good as dead.

And my body would never be found—just like the others.

"It was you—all of you," I said accusingly. My eyes darted from Fenris over to Gunnar and his friend, trying to make my brain remember them from the night between the frat houses. It had to have been them. It made perfect sense. But they were only three, and I'd seen five. I wondered if the other two would be arriving soon.

"We didn't want it to be this way, Eve," Fenris said, his voice full of sadness so thick it was palpable. It clung to me as he did, holding me prisoner. For a second, I believed that he didn't want to be doing what he was doing—that there was true remorse in him for being a party to murder. Then I remembered that it didn't make him any less a killer, and I started screaming like a banshee.

Fenris clamped his hand down over my mouth, but I bit his finger and he yanked it away. One expertly placed elbow in the gut later, I was free from his hold. In fairness, I think I'd surprised him more than hurt him, but I didn't bother asking. Instead, I bolted in the opposite direction, hoping that I could somehow make it to the main road before I was tackled by a killer. Or two.

Maybe three.

"Help me!" I screamed repeatedly, gasping for breath in between. I could hear their footfalls getting closer to me, and they spurred me on, making me dig deeper. Run faster. But Godric had another plan altogether; one I couldn't begin to comprehend. He appeared out of nowhere at the mouth of the alley. He had to have run around the block to cut me off. It seemed like something he would do just to fuck with me. I tried to weave around him, but he caught me with ease, pinning me against the nearest building. He clapped his hand over my mouth, making it hard to breathe. I wondered if that was a small blessing. Maybe I'd pass out before he started stabbing.

"Why are you making this so much harder than it needs to be?" he asked, pressing his heavily muscled body into mine.

"Don't hurt her," Fenris said from somewhere behind me.

A little late for that, don't you think?

"*Godric*," Gunnar said, his commanding tone both notable and unexpected. It made me wonder if he was the one in charge. The one masterminding the whole operation. "You need to—"

An explosion shook the building at my back, knocking me into Godric. We fell together, landing somewhere on the far side of the narrow way. Dust and debris clouded my vision as I tried to get away from my captor; as good a distraction as the blast had been, it made it almost impossible for me to escape. I tried, but I ran into yet another figure looming in the alleyway. His hands clamped down on me like a vise, and I wondered if another of the five had arrived.

"Eve!" Gunnar shouted through the opaque air. I was pretty certain he'd be thrilled when he found out I'd already been caught again.

Asshole.

"You had your chance," a dark voice replied, and I would have sworn the world went quiet around us. Not even the crunch of gravel underfoot sounded in the alley.

"She's ours now, and I think you all know what that means."

The dust began to settle, allowing me to make out the figures around me. There were too many to count, and I closed my eyes, praying that I actually had delved into full-on hallucinations, because that would have been far easier to accept than the reality I was soon to learn.

"*Vega*," Godric snarled somewhere in the distance. "How are you, little brother? I didn't expect to see you so soon."

"Things have changed," my captor replied. "Things are *going* to change even more in the near future." His grip on me tightened, and I cried out in pain.

"This is not your fight, Vega," Gunnar shouted, his voice much closer than before. "It never has been."

"I've made it my fight this time. We all have."

I felt the sharp tip of a blade press against the delicate skin under my ribcage. It was angled up toward my heart. I'd watched enough vampire movies to know that it would be embedded there if he pushed hard enough. And given the strength in his arms as he held me against him, I had little doubt he'd succeed.

With every second, the sun broke through the cloud of dust, giving me a better look at what was in front of me. My eyes went wide when I realized that at least fifty or more new guys had joined us behind the Sketchy Fox, each one of them looking like they belonged on the stage inside.

Each one of them bearing the same dark resemblance to Godric.

"Give her to me, and I'll make it quick," Gunnar said, stepping closer. He, Godric, and Fenris stood shoulder to shoulder, Fenris looking back at the men behind them. "Harm her in any way, and I will draw your death out over centuries."

Centuries...?

I felt the tip of the blade break through my clothes and start to make its way under my skin.

My eyes went wide, silently pleading with Gunnar and Godric to help me. Maybe they were killers, but if they killed guys like the Vega asshole holding onto me, I was okay with that. That whole 'enemy of my enemy is my friend' thing felt appropriate in that moment.

"You can try and kill me once she's gone, but I think you know how it'll end for your kind," Vega said to the guys. "Only ten of you versus thousands of us. Not good odds, even for you."

"No," Godric said, winking at his brother. "Now sounds better."

In a flash, he was in front of me, wrenching the blade away from Vega. As soon as I could no longer feel the point of it in my gut, I bolted toward Gunnar. Yeah, it might not have been a foolproof plan, but we were surrounded by Vega's crew, so it seemed my best option. Gunnar pushed me behind him, wedging me between himself and Fenris. Seconds later, Godric had his back pressed against me as well, the three of them forming a ring around me to keep me safe. My brain was working overtime to try and make sense of this sudden shift in their behavior, but it was distracted by a surge of leather-clad thugs lunging toward us.

I let out a scream.

"Where are the others?" I heard Fenris yell.

"Coming," Gunnar replied, the word little more than a grunt as he parried a blow about to cleave him in half. To say that shit had gotten real would have been an understatement. I had no idea how we were going to get out of there alive.

Eve of Eternal Night

"We need to get her out of here," Fenris growled—and I mean *growled*. He sounded more beast than man.

"We need her to remember," Godric replied, slicing the head off of one of Vega's guys like it was just another day of the week for him. In reality, it probably was, but I decided not to dwell on that fact until later. When I was far, far away from him and his weapons.

When a mob of angry men wasn't trying to kill me.

"Gunnar!" a voice from the far side of the din shouted. Another called out to Fenris. Apparently the cavalry had arrived. I stayed tucked between the three encircling me, jostling from side to side as they battled whoever came for me. I heard a blade slam into something that sounded oddly like cast iron, and I turned to see Fenris look down at his stomach, then lunge toward his attacker, burying his weapon hilt-deep. The eyes of the man about to die turned black as they fell upon me. Then Fenris sliced his head off with one fell swoop.

"Jesus Christ," I gasped, backing into Gunnar.

"Godric!" the therapist who I now highly doubted was a therapist shouted. "Take her!"

"I thought you'd never ask," the dark killer replied.

He dared a glance back at me and flashed a smile that both warmed my insides and chilled me to the bone. The conflict coursing through me was almost enough to distract me from the battle. Reaching back, he grabbed my arm and dragged me out of the safety the three of them had provided. Fenris and Gunnar followed behind to cover our backs while Godric cut a path through the enemy toward the reinforcements.

I cried out in pain as the tip of a knife sliced through my arm. I clamped my hand around it to try and staunch the bleeding, but the cut was deep. If I couldn't get a tourniquet around it, bleeding out was a definite possibility.

The three men now had me penned in against the building wall, working step by step to get us closer to the alley's exit. Though their ability to kill was impressive, I could see the three of them tiring. We weren't going to make it.

"Goddammit, Eve!" Fenris shouted at me. "Why don't you remember?"

"Remember what?" I shouted back. "What am I supposed to remember?"

The sound of blades clanging against one another was my only response.

"Enough of this bullshit," Godric growled. "I'll make her remember whether she likes it or not." He yelled at Gunnar and Fenris to cover him, then fell back behind the tiny wall they'd created between us and the enemy. He looked at me, blue eyes searching mine before he grabbed my face and pulled it close. "I'll have to make this up to you later, too."

Then his lips crashed upon mine, kissing me like a man possessed enough to turn his back on a war just to make out with me. For a fleeting moment, I wanted to push the crazed killer away. But before I could get my hands up to do so, my body was ablaze with desire and recognition and something that felt oddly like love. Like I was living someone else's reaction to him.

And then I realized why. As his tongue forced its way into my mouth, so did memories attached to him. Memories of him on top of me. Memories of a battle not unlike the one we were in. Memories like the vision I'd had of him standing over my dying form. Something in me recognized Godric in a way I couldn't begin to comprehend. All I knew was that it was true and real and so much a part of me that I wondered how I could possibly have been around him and not remembered—even if I couldn't make sense of it.

It was as though we'd lived another life together.

He pulled away from me and stared into my eyes, searching them for some shred of realization. The corner of his mouth curled up when he found what he was looking for.

"I've missed you."

As quickly as he'd kissed me, he was back in the battle. Their numbers must have thinned enough for Fenris and Gunnar to start pressing forward, slicing their way through whoever charged in. Even still, there were a lot of live bodies still in that alley.

"Make a break for it, Fenris," Gunnar shouted. Without pause, my chemistry student who probably wasn't really a student snatched my arm and barreled through the crowd. He didn't even bother using his blade to defend himself, only to attack. I saw him take hits that should have killed him, but he didn't slow. He ran through them no matter what, that cast-iron sound echoing through the narrow passage.

I couldn't see who we were headed for, but I knew we were getting close. I could finally see beyond the battle to the empty street. That nobody had reported us to the cops was shocking—unless it wasn't. The murders I'd previously seen were starting to make a whole lot more sense in a nonsensical kind of way.

Just as we were about to reach the others, I heard a cry of pain from Godric. I dared to look back through the melee. What I saw scared a part of me that I didn't know but couldn't argue with. That part demanded I stop.

That part wouldn't let him die.

With the others embroiled in their own fights, I knew

none of them could get to him fast enough. Vega, his brother—the killer I'd seen in the alcove that night, I realized—and two others had him surrounded. From what I could tell, Godric was unarmed. It was a death sentence at best.

A vision of him on top of me flashed in my mind, and my memories seemed to overtake me. Memories of fighting and killing and loving every second of it. That was what Godric had been saying to me in the alley last night, and I now knew why. He hadn't been trying to scare me. He'd been trying to *reach* me—to reach the part of me that not only understood what was happening, but enjoyed it.

Somewhere deep inside, I loved the thrill of the kill as much as he did.

I ran toward him, scooping up a blade from someone that had fallen along the way. I buried it in the back of one of Vega's men before withdrawing it in a flash and slicing it through the one next to him. That left two against one—Godric and me against Vega.

"You want the pleasure?" I asked Godric, my weapon pointed at Vega.

"I'll take pain and pleasure both," he replied, smiling at me. "But for now, I prefer death."

Before I even realized he'd taken the blade from my hand, it had made its way through Vega's torso. With a violent twist, his brother fell to the ground. I looked around at those still fighting—their numbers thinned to near decimation—and more memories assaulted my mind. Gory, bloody memories played over and over until I had to close my eyes to make them stop. The part of me that knew them warred against the me who was still reeling from the fact that I'd just killed two men to save another that scared me.

Or thrilled me. Or maybe some unhealthy combination of the two.

Sensing my impending meltdown, Godric threw down his weapon and picked me up, pressing me tight against his body. Then he ran through what remained of the fight toward the street. We were in Gunnar's car before the tears started running down my face. It was one thing to think you were going crazy, seeing things that nobody else saw. It was another to realize that you weren't going crazy at all—that instead, the world as you knew it was crumbling around you.

My reality had been shattered with that kiss.

"Don't make me have to knock you out again," he growled, firing up the vehicle. He reached over to brush my hair out of my face, and I cringed away from him. But that place deep inside of me longed to lean into his touch.

"What's happening to me?" I asked, voice shaking with adrenaline.

"You're starting to wake up," he said, letting his hand fall away. If I hadn't seen what Godric was capable of, I would have thought there was a note of sadness in his voice when he said those words. A hint of remorse.

"I don't think I want to," I said softly.

Silence. "You never do, Eve. You never do."

20

———⟨⟨⟨·•·⟩⟩⟩———

Not long after Godric took me home, Gunnar and Fenris arrived. The other two—the ones I hadn't seen yet—were dealing with the mess we'd made, or so Gunnar claimed. Just like they had the night before. Just like they had the night of the Greek Row party. I wondered if they had been the ones to clean up in the alcove that night or if Vega had done so himself. Just another question I needed an answer for.

Learning that I wasn't actually going crazy again made me feel somewhat vindicated, I was still scared shitless. I couldn't deny that something beyond the normal boundaries of reality was going on. That something far beyond my comprehension was afoot.

But I knew they were about to enlighten me regardless.

I sat in the center of my sofa clutching a cushion to my chest, as if that could protect me from what I was about to hear.

"Eve," Gunnar said in his most calm therapist voice. He sat down in the armchair across from me while Godric and Fenris hovered behind him. One looked sad, the other impatient. "What happened today; we can't explain it to you. You have to put it together on your own."

My mouth fell open.

"Are you fucking kidding me?" I launched up out of my seat, throwing the pillow aside. "You drag me back to the scene of the crime I'd just confided in you about, reunite me with the fucking killer himself just before my wannabe boyfriend appears, then all hell breaks loose with demons or whatever the fuck those guys were, and NOW you're telling me that you can't explain?"

My eyes flashed over to Fenris, who winced at my words.

"We can't," he said softly. "That's how it works."

"What were those guys? Because they sure as fuck weren't human."

Nobody replied.

"Are you? Are you three human?"

They didn't move.

"Am I?" Their silence made me itchy. I stepped around Gunnar to thrust my finger into Godric's chest. "What did you do to my head? Why am I seeing you and me in some sort of weird past war or whatever? Are you a... a *wizard* or something?"

That cocky bastard actually laughed. "I am most certainly not a wizard."

"Then what are you, and what did you do to me... when you kissed me?" Though I hated myself for it, I could feel my cheeks flush with the mere mention of what he'd done to me against that building. The heat I felt made no sense, but I reacted anyway.

"I sparked your magic, that's all. What you saw was yours to see."

So not helpful.

"What exactly *did* you see?" Gunnar asked, standing up beside me.

"I saw him," I replied, pointing at Godric. "He was dressed weird—in some kind of old combat gear or something. Some kind of armor. He was covered in blood and smiling at me. I don't know what I was doing—the vision was in first person so I couldn't actually see myself."

"Is that all you saw?" Godric asked, quirking a brow at me.

My cheeks grew redder by the second. "No. I saw other stuff."

"What kind of stuff?" he asked, stepping closer to me until his body brushed up against mine.

"Not battle-related stuff." I quickly turned my attention to Fenris and Gunnar, who stood by quietly. "I didn't see either of you."

"You wouldn't have," Fenris replied, as if somehow that was supposed to make all the sense in the world.

"What. Kind. Of. Stuff?" Godric repeated, clipping his words with irritation in his tone.

"Sex, okay? I saw you naked on top of me, grinning like a psychopath." He smiled down at me—the very same expression I'd seen in my vision. "Yeah. That's the smile."

"So you really do remember," he said, his voice low and husky. He pressed against me harder, the length of his body molded to mine. My heart sped up as his hands cupped my waist, making sure I could feel just how happy he was to learn that I'd remembered that little tidbit. I, however, was still freaked out by it. Turned on, but freaked out all the same.

"I saw pieces of a puzzle that I can't put together. That's what I saw."

"Apparently you needed a little stimulation to make you

remember this time," Godric said, angling his head to kiss me. "Maybe you just need a little more."

His lips pressed against mine, and the second they did, my mind exploded with more visions. More memories. More death and blood and sex.

And wings... Godric stood before me, wings as black as night spread wide behind him.

I pulled away, breathing hard and staring at him.

"You're an angel." I said it as though it were an accusation.

"A dark angel," he replied. That distinction appeared to be important to him.

"Vega and the others," I started, trying to puzzle it out. "They're like you."

He nodded. "They are the enemy."

"And you?" I turned to Fenris, eyes wide with disbelief.

"I'm not that," was his only reply.

"Gunnar?"

"I'm not either."

"What the fuck are you two, then?" Silence. "You can't say, can you?" They both shook their heads. "Fine. Then tell me why those dark angels clearly wanted me dead." I turned back to Godric. "And why you don't."

I swear he looked like I'd slapped him with that question. "That we cannot say either. Not until you remember everything."

"Okay, then how do I do that? Because this in-between is starting to make me feel insane again."

"You're not insane," Gunnar replied, his tone full of sympathy.

"I know that now, no thanks to you."

"I could not tell you. I did my best to find a way to force your mind to see the truth."

"Epic fail, Freddie. Epic fucking fail."

He pulled me from Godric's hold and spun me to face him, lowering his face until it was only inches from mine. I gasped, startled by his abrupt behavior. But when I looked into his hazel eyes, I felt a pull that I couldn't deny. The same kind that I'd felt with Godric that night in the bar when he'd touched me. Color returned to my cheeks in a hurry the longer he stared at me.

"You can feel that, can't you?" he asked. "The pull between us?"

"I feel confused and tired," I replied, wiggling out of his grip. "And I wish someone could just tell me what's going on!"

"Eve," Fenris called softly, pushing past Gunnar to stand in front of me. He wove his arms around my neck and pulled me into his embrace. "I'm so sorry about last night—and this morning, for that matter. I know you're scared and you don't want to show it. I know you feel like you're on the brink of losing it again. Just know that we're here for you. That you need us—that you're *supposed* to need us. That's why you feel the way you do when we're around." He pushed me away just enough to look down at me with those baby blue eyes that made my stomach do a little flip. "Don't fight it. We can't help you if you fight it."

"Fight *what*?" I asked, growing more and more frustrated by the second.

Fenris cupped my face, stroking my cheek with the pad of his thumb.

"This..."

Without warning, he bent down and brushed his lips against mine, slowly stoking a fire inside me that came out of nowhere. One second I was getting angry, the next I was putty in his hands. I leaned into his kiss, letting him have his way with me. I didn't care that Gunnar and Godric were watching, or that earlier that day I'd thought he'd betrayed me. All I cared about was the spark between us, and the memories tugging at my mind.

Instead of a barrage of clips like I'd seen with Godric, this time I saw one complete memory play out; one of Fenris, asking me for orders in a language that I seemed to understand. He wanted to know how to proceed with the mission we were on. I barked out a response in the same tongue, and he nodded at me before storming off toward a valley in the distance where I could see a handful of others already embattled. My fiery red hair blew around me wildly as I looked down at the fight being waged and Fenris running toward it. Midway there, he leapt into the air, his body morphing into something massive and furry. He landed with a thud that shook the ground I stood on, then looked back over his shoulder at me. I let out a battle cry that made present-time me break out in goosebumps. That sound reverberated in my mind with such clarity, bringing me back to that moment as if I were about to relive it.

With a gasp, I pulled away from Fenris, staring up at him.

"You're a wolf..."

"Yes." His smile was bigger than I'd ever seen it.

"You kill for me," I said, my voice husky and low.

"*Always*," he replied with a growl that sounded as inhuman as he was.

My mind was still reeling when Gunnar put his hand on my shoulder and turned me to face him. The second he made contact, that feeling—the one he'd brought to my attention—felt even stronger. Like a part of him was begging me to come to him. To remember.

"Eve." He said my name like it was sacred to him. "Don't be afraid."

And I wasn't. I should have been. I should have been scared shitless, but I wasn't. Something about staring into his eyes gave me comfort unlike any other had ever provided.

He stepped closer to me, carefully assessing my reaction the entire time. When I stood my ground against him, he let a tiny smile tug at the corner of his mouth.

"Always so brave," he murmured, running his hand through my hair until he cupped the back of my head. "Our fearless leader."

Fearless what?

I didn't get a chance to ask that question because Gunnar's soft lips were forcing mine open with a determination that I was loath to fight. I let him in, sinking deeper and deeper into the past with every stroke of his tongue. I saw flashes of him and me together—suiting up for war. Discussing strategy. Burying our dead. Side by side, we faced horrors together, and I could feel his allegiance through those memories—how important he was to me.

His lips were ripped away from mine abruptly, and I looked up to see Godric holding him back from me. I could see plainly from Gunnar's expression that he hadn't been ready to stop just yet. There was a shadow in his eyes that alerted some part of my brain to a dissonance within the group. A rivalry I didn't understand but could clearly feel.

"Hey!" I shouted, and both of their heads snapped to mine. "That's enough." Godric dropped his hands from Gunnar and walked toward me, taking his place beside me. I pretended I didn't notice when his palm landed on the small of my back. "I still have questions," I said, looking at each of them in turn. "I think someone needs to make breakfast. It's going to be a long morning."

 ❧

AND IT WAS.

Hours of fruitless interrogation later, I felt no closer to understanding what was going on. I could see that the inability to tell me anything helpful pained the trio, but that didn't make me feel much better. I needed answers, not guilt. The three of them refused to leave me, so I eventually took refuge from our frustrating conversation in my bedroom. Godric lingered in my doorway, hunger in his eyes, until I kicked him out to the living room. I flopped down on my bed, playing the events of the last few days over and over in my mind. All it left me with was more unanswered questions. How did I know these guys? And when did I know them? It was clear it hadn't been in this lifetime. And why were we constantly fighting in my memories? *Who* exactly were we fighting?

Then my mind turned to the dark angels.

During the fight, Gunnar, Godric, and Fenris had seemed so surprised by their presence—like they hadn't expected to see them there. Or at all, for that matter. In all the fragmented memories that had returned, I didn't remember seeing them once. It was always other warriors I saw. And a girl...

In the memory where Fenris had changed into a wolf before my very eyes, there had been a girl in the distance, her long blonde hair blowing as wildly as mine had. Something about her made anger stir within me, a wild storm rolling closer to the surface with every second I thought of her. Something deep within me recognized her in a visceral way.

And it hated her.

But how did all these pieces fit together? That was the most important question of all—the most pressing and elusive one. If the three of them couldn't—or wouldn't—tell me, then I needed to hunt down the missing two and use them to help regain more of my memory. And I had a pretty good idea how. Iver and Stian knew each other and were working together. They'd also appeared around the same time as the others.

Playing the one-sided conversation I'd overheard outside of Iver's office over in my mind, I could see it for what it was: a plot to get me to remember. I wondered which of the others had been talking to him that day, trying to figure out how to get to me before Vega and his boys did. If I'd been a betting girl, I would have put my money on Gunnar.

Regardless of who it was, I knew I wouldn't have to look any further than Iver and Stian to find the missing pieces of the puzzle. I planned to track them down first thing in the morning. In the meantime, I would stay close to Gunnar, Godric, and Fenris, just in case any other dark angels came for me.

And I'd sleep with a blade tucked snugly under my pillow.

A girl can never be too careful.

THE ZODIAC CURSE CONTINUES

ABOUT THE AUTHOR

AMBER LYNN NATUSCH is the author of the bestselling *Caged*, as well as the *Light and Shadow* series with Shannon Morton. She was born and raised in Winnipeg, and speaks sarcasm fluently because of her Canadian roots. She loves to dance and sing in her kitchen—much to the detriment of those near her—but spends most of her time running a practice with her husband, raising two small children, and attempting to write when she can lock herself in the bathroom for ten minutes of peace and quiet. She has many hidden talents, most of which should not be mentioned but include putting her foot in her mouth, acting inappropriately when nervous, swearing like a sailor when provoked, and not listening when she should. She's obsessed with home renovation shows, should never be caffeinated, and loves snow. Amber has a deep-seated fear of clowns and deep water...especially clowns swimming in deep water.

http://amberlynnnatusch.com